Note

KING LEAR was most likely written sometime in 1605 and was first performed at court in 1606. The play is considered by many to be the finest tragedy by Shakespeare (1564–1616) and certainly among the most powerful in Western literature. The story of King Lear has its roots in ancient Celtic legend, and is included in Geoffrey of Monmouth's *Historia Regum Britanniae* (c. 1136). However, in Monmouth's version, Lear is reunited with Cordelia and restored to his throne with the help of her husband, Aganippus, King of the Franks. This happy ending is similar to that of *The True Chronicle History of King Leir*, the most immediate source of Shakespeare's play, published in 1605. It has been suggested that Shakespeare's tragic ending was perhaps derived from the source of the Edmund-Edgar-Gloucester subplot, Philip Sidney's *Arcadia* (1590).

Shakespeare's finale, however, was too bleak for later audiences, particularly in the eighteenth century when the play's ending was altered to conform to that Age's desire for reason and order. For many eighteenth-century critics, Lear's madness was a curse rather than the "Reason in madness" perceived by the play's other "madman," Edgar; it wasn't until 1838 that the Shakespearean ending was restored. For today's audience, *King Lear* and Shakespeare's tragic vision echo the classic view that enlightenment comes only through suffering. That Lear dies and that Cordelia is sacrificed for Lear's education becomes secondary to the fact that he at last obtains self-knowledge.

DOVER · THRIFT · EDITIONS

King Lear

WILLIAM SHAKESPEARE

DOVER PUBLICATIONS, INC.
New York

DOVER THRIFT EDITIONS

GENERAL EDITOR: STANLEY APPELBAUM
EDITOR OF THIS VOLUME: CANDACE WARD

Performance

This Dover Thrift Edition may be used in its entirety, in adaptation or in any other way for theatrical productions, professional and amateur, in the United States, without fee, permission or acknowledgment. (This may not apply outside of the United States, as copyright conditions may vary.)

Copyright

Bibliographical Note

This Dover edition, first published in 1994, contains the unabridged text of *King Lear* as published in Volume XVII of *The Caxton Edition of the Complete Works of William Shakespeare,* Caxton Publishing Company, London, n.d. The Note and explanatory footnotes were prepared specially for this edition.

Library of Congress Cataloging-in-Publication Data

Shakespeare, William, 1564–1616.
    King Lear / William Shakespeare.
        p.   cm. — (Dover thrift editions)
    ISBN 0-486-28058-6 (pbk.)
    1. Lear, King (Legendary character) — Drama.   I. Title.   II. Series.
PR2819.A1   1994
822.3'3 — dc20   93–41036
                                                                        CIP

Manufactured in the United States of America
Dover Publications, Inc., 31 East 2nd Street, Mineola, N.Y. 11501

Contents

Dramatis Personæ

LEAR, King of Britain.
KING OF FRANCE.
DUKE OF BURGUNDY.
DUKE OF CORNWALL.
DUKE OF ALBANY.
EARL OF KENT.
EARL OF GLOUCESTER.
EDGAR, *son to Gloucester.*
EDMUND, *bastard son to Gloucester.*
CURAN, *a courtier.*
Old Man, *tenant to Gloucester.*
Doctor.
Fool.
OSWALD, *steward to Goneril.*
A Captain employed by Edmund.
Gentleman attendant on Cordelia.
A Herald.
Servants to Cornwall.

GONERIL,
REGAN, } *daughters to Lear.*
CORDELIA,

Knights of Lear's train, Captains,
    Messengers, Soldiers, *and* Attendants.

ACT I

SCENE I — *King Lear's Palace*

Enter KENT, GLOUCESTER, *and* EDMUND

KENT.   I thought the king had more affected[1] the Duke of Albany than Cornwall.

GLOU.   It did always seem so to us: but now, in the division of the kingdom, it appears not which of the dukes he values most; for equalities are so weighed that curiosity in neither can make choice of either's moiety.[2]

KENT.   Is not this your son, my lord?

GLOU.   His breeding, sir, hath been at my charge: I have so often blushed to acknowledge him that now I am brazed[3] to it.

KENT.   I cannot conceive[4] you.

GLOU.   Sir, this young fellow's mother could: whereupon she grew round-wombed, and had indeed, sir, a son for her cradle ere she had a husband for her bed. Do you smell a fault?

KENT.   I cannot wish the fault undone, the issue of it being so proper.[5]

GLOU.   But I have, sir, a son by order of law, some year elder than this, who yet is no dearer in my account: though this knave came something saucily into the world before he was sent for, yet was his mother fair; there was good sport at his making, and the whoreson must be acknowledged. Do you know this noble gentleman, Edmund?

---

1. *more affected*] showed greater affection for.
2. *moiety*] portion, part.
3. *brazed*] brazened, hardened.
4. *conceive*] understand.
5. *proper*] goodly, handsome.

1

EDM.   No, my lord.

GLOU.   My lord of Kent: remember him hereafter as my honourable
    friend.

EDM.   My services to your lordship.

KENT.   I must love you, and sue[6] to know you better.

EDM.   Sir, I shall study deserving.[7]

GLOU.   He hath been out nine years, and away he shall again. The
    king is coming.

Sennet.[8] *Enter one bearing a coronet,* KING LEAR, CORNWALL, ALBANY,
GONERIL, REGAN, CORDELIA, *and* Attendants

LEAR.   Attend the lords of France and Burgundy, Gloucester.

GLOU.   I shall, my liege.   [*Exeunt Gloucester and Edmund.*]

LEAR.   Meantime we shall express our darker purpose.
    Give me the map there. Know we have divided
    In three our kingdom: and 't is our fast[9] intent
    To shake all cares and business from our age,
    Conferring them on younger strengths, while we
    Unburthen'd crawl toward death. Our son of Cornwall,
    And you, our no less loving son of Albany,
    We have this hour a constant will to publish
    Our daughters' several dowers, that future strife
    May be prevented now. The princes, France and Burgundy,
    Great rivals in our youngest daughter's love,
    Long in our court have made their amorous sojourn,
    And here are to be answer'd. Tell me, my daughters,
    Since now we will divest us both of rule,
    Interest of territory,[10] cares of state,
    Which of you shall we say doth love us most?
    That we our largest bounty may extend
    Where nature doth with merit challenge.[11] Goneril,
    Our eldest-born, speak first.

---

6. *sue*] beg, entreat.
7. *study deserving*] study to be worthy (of your acquaintance).
8. *Sennet*] a note of music commonly indicating the entrance or exit of important charac-
ters.
9. *fast*] firmly fixed.
10. *Interest of territory*] profit derived from possession of territory.
11. *Where nature . . . challenge*] Where natural affection prefers a claim equally with merit,
where the due of natural affection coincides with the due of merit.

GON.   Sir, I love you more than words can wield the matter,
           Dearer than eye-sight, space and liberty,
           Beyond what can be valued, rich or rare,
           No less than life, with grace, health, beauty, honour,
           As much as child e'er loved or father found;
           A love that makes breath poor and speech unable;
           Beyond all manner of so much I love you.
COR.   [*Aside*] What shall Cordelia do? Love, and be silent.
LEAR.   Of all these bounds, even from this line to this,
           With shadowy forests and with champains[12] rich'd,
           With plenteous rivers and wide-skirted meads,
           We make thee lady. To thine and Albany's issue
           Be this perpetual. What says our second daughter,
           Our dearest Regan, wife to Cornwall? Speak.
REG.   I am made of that self[13] metal as my sister,
           And prize me at her worth. In my true heart
           I find she names my very deed of love;
           Only she comes too short: that I profess
           Myself an enemy to all other joys
           Which the most precious square of sense possesses,[14]
           And find I am alone felicitate[15]
           In your dear highness' love.
COR.   [*Aside*] Then poor Cordelia!
           And yet not so, since I am sure my love's
           More ponderous than my tongue.
LEAR.   To thee and thine hereditary ever
           Remain this ample third of our fair kingdom,
           No less in space, validity and pleasure,
           Than that conferr'd on Goneril. Now, our joy,
           Although the last, not least, to whose young love
           The vines of France and milk of Burgundy
           Strive to be interess'd,[16] what can you say to draw
           A third more opulent than your sisters? Speak.

---

12. *champains*] open country.
13. *self*] self-same.
14. *most . . . possesses*] i.e., which the soundest sense acknowledges as joy.
15. *felicitate*] made happy.
16. *to be interess'd*] to establish a claim, right.

COR.	Nothing, my lord.
LEAR.	Nothing!
COR.	Nothing.
LEAR.	Nothing will come of nothing: speak again.
COR.	Unhappy that I am, I cannot heave
	My heart into my mouth: I love your majesty
	According to my bond;[17] nor more nor less.
LEAR.	How, how, Cordelia! mend your speech a little,
	Lest it mar your fortunes.
COR.	Good my lord,
	You have begot me, bred me, loved me: I
	Return those duties back as are right fit,
	Obey you, love you, and most honour you.
	Why have my sisters husbands, if they say
	They love you all? Haply, when I shall wed,
	That lord whose hand must take my plight shall carry
	Half my love with him, half my care and duty:
	Sure, I shall never marry like my sisters,
	To love my father all.
LEAR.	But goes thy heart with this?
COR.	Ay, good my lord.
LEAR.	So young, and so untender?
COR.	So young, my lord, and true.
LEAR.	Let it be so; thy truth then be thy dower:
	For, by the sacred radiance of the sun,
	The mysteries of Hecate, and the night;
	By all the operation of the orbs
	From whom we do exist and cease to be;
	Here I disclaim all my paternal care,
	Propinquity and property of blood,
	And as a stranger to my heart and me
	Hold thee from this for ever. The barbarous Scythian,[18]
	Or he that makes his generation messes[19]
	To gorge his appetite, shall to my bosom

---

17. *According to my bond*] According to my duty as your daughter.
18. *Scythian*] the inhabitants of Scythia, part of what was Russia, were considered the extreme types of barbarity.
19. *he that . . . messes*] he that makes meals of his children.

	Be as well neighbour'd, pitied and relieved,
	As thou my sometime daughter.
KENT.	Good my liege, —
LEAR.	Peace, Kent!
	Come not between the dragon and his wrath.
	I loved her most, and thought to set my rest
	On her kind nursery. Hence, and avoid my sight!
	So be my grave my peace, as here I give
	Her father's heart from her! Call France. Who stirs?
	Call Burgundy. Cornwall and Albany.
	With my two daughters' dowers digest[20] this third:
	Let pride, which she calls plainness, marry her.
	I do invest you jointly with my power,
	Pre-eminence and all the large effects[21]
	That troop with majesty. Ourself, by monthly course,
	With reservation of an hundred knights
	By you to be sustain'd, shall our abode
	Make with you by due turns. Only we still retain
	The name and all the additions to a king;[22]
	The sway, revenue, execution of the rest,
	Beloved sons, be yours: which to confirm,
	This coronet part betwixt you.
KENT.	Royal Lear,
	Whom I have ever honour'd as my king,
	Loved as my father, as my master follow'd,
	As my great patron thought on in my prayers, —
LEAR.	The bow is bent and drawn; make from the shaft.[23]
KENT.	Let it fall rather, though the fork[24] invade
	The region of my heart: be Kent unmannerly,
	When Lear is mad. What wouldst thou do, old man?
	Think'st thou that duty shall have dread to speak,
	When power to flattery bows? To plainness honour's bound,
	When majesty stoops to folly. Reverse thy doom,

---

20. *digest*] absorb.
21. *the large effects*] the spacious attributes or dignities.
22. *additions to a king*] titles of a king.
23. *make from the shaft*] take the risk, come what may (Lear is telling Kent, now that he's gone so far, to finish his speech).
24. *fork*] arrowhead.

	And in thy best consideration check
	This hideous rashness: answer my life my judgement,
	Thy youngest daughter does not love thee least;
	Nor are those empty-hearted whose low sound
	Reverbs no hollowness.[25]

LEAR.   Kent, on thy life, no more.

KENT.   My life I never held but as a pawn
        To wage against thy enemies, nor fear to lose it,
        Thy safety being the motive.

LEAR.   Out of my sight!

KENT.   See better, Lear, and let me still remain
        The true blank[26] of thine eye.

LEAR.   Now, by Apollo, —

KENT.   Now, by Apollo, king,
        Thou swear'st thy gods in vain.

LEAR.   O, vassal! miscreant!

                          [*Laying his hand on his sword.*]

ALB.
CORN.   } Dear sir, forbear.

KENT.   Do;
        Kill thy physician, and the fee bestow
        Upon the foul disease. Revoke thy doom;
        Or, whilst I can vent clamour from my throat,
        I'll tell thee thou dost evil.

LEAR.   Hear me, recreant!
        On thy allegiance, hear me!
        Since thou hast sought to make us break our vow,
        Which we durst never yet, and with strain'd pride
        To come between our sentence and our power,
        Which nor our nature nor our place can bear,
        Our potency made good, take thy reward.
        Five days we do allot thee, for provision
        To shield thee from diseases[27] of the world,
        And on the sixth to turn thy hated back

---

25. *Reverbs no hollowness*] reverberates no insincerity or emptiness.
26. *blank*] The white mark forming the bull's eye of the target. Kent appeals to Lear to let
    him remain by him as the mark by which to guide the aim of his vision.
27. *diseases*] troubles, distresses.

          Upon our kingdom: if on the tenth day following
          Thy banish'd trunk be found in our dominions,
          The moment is thy death. Away! By Jupiter,
          This shall not be revoked.
KENT.   Fare thee well, king: sith[28] thus thou wilt appear,
          Freedom lives hence,[29] and banishment is here.
          [*To Cordelia*] The gods to their dear shelter take thee, maid,
          That justly think'st and hast most rightly said!
          [*To Regan and Goneril*] And your large speeches may your
              deeds approve,
          That good effects may spring from words of love.
          Thus Kent, O princes, bids you all adieu;
          He'll shape his old course in a country new.   [*Exit.*]

Flourish. Re-enter GLOUCESTER, *with* FRANCE, BURGUNDY, *and* Attendants

GLOU.   Here's France and Burgundy, my noble lord.
LEAR.   My lord of Burgundy,
          We first address towards you, who with this king
          Hath rivall'd for our daughter: what, in the least,
          Will you require in present dower with her,
          Or cease your quest of love?
BUR.   Most royal majesty,
          I crave no more than what your highness offer'd,
          Nor will you tender less.
LEAR.   Right noble Burgundy,
          When she was dear to us, we did hold her so;
          But now her price is fall'n. Sir, there she stands:
          If aught within that little seeming substance,
          Or all of it, with our displeasure pieced,[30]
          And nothing more, may fitly like your grace,
          She's there, and she is yours.
BUR.   I know no answer.
LEAR.   Will you, with those infirmities she owes,[31]

---

  28. *sith*] since, seeing that.
  29. *hence*] not here, at a distance.
  30. *pieced*] supplemented.
  31. *owes*] has, possesses.

	Unfriended, new adopted to our hate,
	Dower'd with our curse and stranger'd with our oath,[32]
	Take her, or leave her?
BUR.	Pardon me, royal sir;
	Election makes not up on[33] such conditions.
LEAR.	Then leave her, sir; for, by the power that made me,

I tell you all her wealth. [*To France*] For you, great king,
I would not from your love make such a stray,
To match[34] you where I hate; therefore beseech you
To avert your liking a more worthier way
Than on a wretch whom nature is ashamed
Almost to acknowledge hers.

FRANCE.   This is most strange,
That she, that even but now was your best object,
The argument of your praise, balm of your age,
Most best, most dearest, should in this trice of time
Commit a thing so monstrous, to dismantle
So many folds of favour. Sure, her offence
Must be of such unnatural degree
That monsters it, or your fore-vouch'd affection
Fall'n into taint:[35] which to believe of her,
Must be a faith that reason without miracle
Could never plant in me.

COR.   I yet beseech your majesty, —
If for I want that glib and oily art,
To speak and purpose not, since what I well intend,
I'll do't before I speak, — that you make known
It is no vicious blot, murder, or foulness,
No unchaste action, or dishonour'd step,
That hath deprived me of your grace and favour;
But even for want of that for which I am richer,
A still-soliciting eye,[36] and such a tongue

---

32. *stranger'd . . . oath*] made a stranger to us, alienated from us by oath.
33. *Election makes not up*] No choice is possible.
34. *I would not. . . . To match*] I would not neglect or ignore your love to such an extent as to match. . . .
35. *her offence . . . taint*] Cordelia's offence must have been extremely monstrous to have caused Lear's previous affection to become tainted.
36. *still-soliciting*] constantly importuning.

As I am glad I have not, though not to have it
Hath lost me in your liking.

LEAR.   Better thou
Hadst not been born than not to have pleased me better.

FRANCE.   Is it but this? a tardiness in nature
Which often leaves the history unspoke
That it intends to do? My lord of Burgundy,
What say you to the lady? Love's not love
When it is mingled with regards that stand
Aloof from the entire point.[37] Will you have her?
She is herself a dowry.

BUR.   Royal Lear,
Give but that portion which yourself proposed,
And here I take Cordelia by the hand,
Duchess of Burgundy.

LEAR.   Nothing: I have sworn; I am firm.

BUR.   I am sorry then you have so lost a father
That you must lose a husband.

COR.   Peace be with Burgundy!
Since that respects[38] of fortune are his love,
I shall not be his wife.

FRANCE.   Fairest Cordelia, that art most rich being poor,
Most choice forsaken, and most loved despised,
Thee and thy virtues here I seize upon:
Be it lawful I take up what's cast away.
Gods, gods! 't is strange that from their cold'st neglect
My love should kindle to inflamed respect.
Thy dowerless daughter, king, thrown to my chance,
Is queen of us, of ours, and our fair France:
Not all the dukes of waterish[39] Burgundy
Can buy this unprized[40] precious maid of me.
Bid them farewell, Cordelia, though unkind:
Thou losest here, a better where to find.

------

37. *with regards . . . the entire point*] with scruples that are irrelevant to the essential or main
point.
38. *respects*] considerations.
39. *waterish*] well-watered.
40. *unprized*] priceless.

LEAR. Thou hast her, France: let her be thine, for we
    Have no such daughter, nor shall ever see
    That face of hers again. Therefore be gone
    Without our grace, our love, our benison.[41]
    Come, noble Burgundy.
   [Flourish. Exeunt all but France, Goneril, Regan, and Cordelia.]
FRANCE. Bid farewell to your sisters.
COR. The jewels of our father, with wash'd eyes
    Cordelia leaves you: I know you what you are;
    And, like a sister, am most loath to call
    Your faults as they are named. Use well our father:
    To your professed bosoms I commit him:
    But yet, alas, stood I within his grace,
    I would prefer him to a better place.
    So farewell to you both.
REG. Prescribe not us our duties.
GON.   Let your study
    Be to content your lord, who hath received you
    At fortune's alms. You have obedience scanted,
    And well are worth the want that you have wanted.[42]
COR. Time shall unfold what plaited cunning hides:
    Who cover faults, at last shame them derides.[43]
    Well may you prosper!
FRANCE.   Come, my fair Cordelia.
         [Exeunt France and Cordelia.]
GON. Sister, it is not a little I have to say of what most nearly appertains to us both. I think our father will hence to-night.
REG. That's most certain, and with you; next month with us.
GON. You see how full of changes his age is; the observation we have made of it hath not been little: he always loved our sister most; and with what poor judgement he hath now cast her off appears too grossly.
REG. 'T is the infirmity of his age: yet he hath ever but slenderly known himself.

---

41. *benison*] blessing.
42. *well . . . wanted*] well deserve to suffer the want of that affection (from your husband) which you have shown yourself to be without (for your father).
43. *Who . . . derides*] Shame will eventually deride those who try to hide their faults.

GON.   The best and soundest of his time hath been but rash; then
          must we look to receive from his age, not alone the imperfections of
          long ingrafted condition, but therewithal the unruly waywardness
          that infirm and choleric years bring with them.
REG.   Such unconstant starts are we like to have from him as this of
          Kent's banishment.
GON.   There is further compliment of leave-taking between France
          and him. Pray you, let's hit together: if our father carry authority
          with such dispositions as he bears, this last surrender of his will but
          offend us.⁴⁴
REG.   We shall further think on 't.
GON.   We must do something, and i' the heat.⁴⁵   [*Exeunt.*]

SCENE II — *The Earl of Gloucester's Castle*

Enter EDMUND, *with a letter*

EDM.   Thou, nature, art my goddess; to thy law
          My services are bound. Wherefore should I
          Stand in the plague of custom, and permit
          The curiosity of nations to deprive me,
          For that I am some twelve or fourteen moonshines
          Lag of a brother? Why bastard? wherefore base?¹
          When my dimensions are as well compact,²
          My mind as generous and my shape as true,

---

44. *let's hit together . . . offend us*] let's join together in our course of action; if our father
    asserts his authority in such headstrong temper as he now shows, this final surrender to
    us of his kingdom will merely breed trouble for us.
45. *i' the heat*] now; as in the proverb, "Strike while the iron's hot."

---

 1. *Lag of a brother*] Lagging behind a brother, i.e., older than my brother.
    base] "A *base* son" was a synonym for "a bastard." The words have no etymological
    connection.
 2. *my dimensions . . . compact*] my proportions are put together as well.

As honest madam's issue? Why brand they us
With base? with baseness? bastardy? base, base?
Who in the lusty stealth of nature take
More composition[3] and fierce quality
Than doth, within a dull, stale, tired bed,
Go to the creating a whole tribe of fops,
Got 'tween asleep and wake? Well then,
Legitimate Edgar, I must have your land:
Our father's love is to the bastard Edmund
As to the legitimate: fine word, "legitimate"!
Well, my legitimate, if this letter speed
And my invention thrive, Edmund the base
Shall top the legitimate. I grow; I prosper:
Now, gods, stand up for bastards!

Enter GLOUCESTER

GLOU.   Kent banish'd thus! and France in choler parted!
And the king gone to-night! subscribed[4] his power!
Confined to exhibition![5] All this done
Upon the gad! Edmund, how now! what news?
EDM.   So please your lordship, none.   *[Putting up the letter.]*
GLOU.   Why so earnestly seek you to put up that letter?
EDM.   I know no news, my lord.
GLOU.   What paper were you reading?
EDM.   Nothing, my lord.
GLOU.   No? What needed then that terrible dispatch of it into your pocket? the quality of nothing hath not such need to hide itself. Let's see: come, if it be nothing, I shall not need spectacles.
EDM.   I beseech you, sir, pardon me: it is a letter from my brother, that I have not all o'er-read; and for so much as I have perused, I find it not fit for your o'er-looking.
GLOU.   Give me the letter, sir.
EDM.   I shall offend, either to detain or give it. The contents, as in part I understand them, are to blame.

---

3. *More composition*] More effective blending.
4. *subscribed*] yielded (by a written surrender).
5. *Confined to exhibition*] Restricted to an allowance.

GLOU.   Let's see, let's see.

EDM.   I hope, for my brother's justification, he wrote this but as an essay or taste[6] of my virtue.

GLOU.   [*Reads*]:

"This policy and reverence of age makes the world bitter to the best of our times; keeps our fortunes from us till our oldness cannot relish them. I begin to find an idle and fond[7] bondage in the oppression of aged tyranny; who sways, not as it hath power, but as it is suffered. Come to me, that of this I may speak more. If our father would sleep till I waked him, you should enjoy half his revenue for ever, and live the beloved of your brother,

                                                        EDGAR.

Hum! Conspiracy! — "Sleep till I waked him, you should enjoy half his revenue!" — My son Edgar! Had he a hand to write this? a heart and brain to breed it in? When came this to you? who brought it?

EDM.   It was not brought me, my lord; there's the cunning of it; I found it thrown in at the casement of my closet.

GLOU.   You know the character[8] to be your brother's?

EDM.   If the matter were good, my lord, I durst swear it were his; but, in respect of that, I would fain think it were not.

GLOU.   It is his.

EDM.   It is his hand, my lord; but I hope his heart is not in the contents.

GLOU.   Hath he never heretofore sounded you in this business?

EDM.   Never, my lord: but I have heard him oft maintain it to be fit, that, sons at perfect age, and fathers declining, the father should be as ward to the son, and the son manage his revenue.

GLOU.   O villain, villain! His very opinion in the letter! Abhorred villain! Unnatural, detested, brutish villain! worse than brutish! Go, sirrah, seek him; ay, apprehend him: abominable villain! Where is he?

EDM.   I do not well know, my lord. If it shall please you to suspend your indignation against my brother till you can derive from him

---

6. *essay or taste*] trial or test.
7. *fond*] foolish.
8. *character*] handwriting.

better testimony of his intent, you should run a certain course; where, if you violently proceed against him, mistaking his purpose, it would make a great gap in your own honour and shake in pieces the heart of his obedience. I dare pawn down my life for him that he hath wrote this to feel my affection to your honour and to no further pretence of danger.

GLOU.   Think you so?

EDM.   If your honour judge it meet, I will place you where you shall hear us confer of this, and by an auricular assurance have your satisfaction, and that without any further delay than this very evening.

GLOU.   He cannot be such a monster —

EDM.   Nor is not, sure.

GLOU.   To his father, that so tenderly and entirely loves him. Heaven and earth! Edmund, seek him out; wind me into him, I pray you: frame the business after your own wisdom. I would unstate myself, to be in a due resolution.[9]

EDM.   I will seek him, sir, presently, convey[10] the business as I shall find means, and acquaint you withal.

GLOU.   These late eclipses in the sun and moon portend no good to us: though the wisdom of nature can reason it thus and thus, yet nature finds itself scourged by the sequent effects: love cools, friendship falls off, brothers divide: in cities, mutinies; in countries, discord; in palaces, treason; and the bond cracked 'twixt son and father. This villain of mine comes under the prediction; there's son against father: the king falls from bias of nature; there's father against child. We have seen the best of our time: machinations, hollowness, treachery and all ruinous disorders follow us disquietly to our graves. Find out this villain, Edmund; it shall lose thee nothing; do it carefully. And the noble and true-hearted Kent banished! his offence, honesty! 'T is strange.   [*Exit.*]

EDM.   This is the excellent foppery of the world, that when we are

---

9. *I would unstate . . . resolution*] I would give up my rank and estate in order to assure myself (of the facts).

10. *convey*] tactfully manage.

sick in fortune — often the surfeit[11] of our own behaviour — we make guilty of our disasters the sun, the moon and the stars: as if we were villains by necessity, fools by heavenly compulsion; knaves, thieves and treachers, by spherical predominance; drunkards, liars and adulterers, by an enforced obedience of planetary influence; and all that we are evil in, by a divine thrusting on: an admirable evasion of whoremaster man, to lay his goatish disposition to the charge of a star! My father compounded with my mother under the dragon's tail, and my nativity was under Ursa major; so that it follows I am rough and lecherous. Tut, I should have been that I am, had the maidenliest star in the firmament twinkled on my bastardizing. Edgar —

Enter EDGAR

And pat he comes like the catastrophe of the old comedy:[12] my cue is villanous melancholy, with a sigh like Tom o' Bedlam.[13] O, these eclipses do portend these divisions! fa, sol, la, mi.

EDG.   How now, brother Edmund! what serious contemplation are you in?

EDM.   I am thinking, brother, of a prediction I read this other day, what should follow these eclipses.

EDG.   Do you busy yourself about that?

EDM.   I promise you, the effects he writ of succeed unhappily; as of unnaturalness between the child and the parent; death, dearth, dissolutions of ancient amities; divisions in state, menaces and maledictions against king and nobles; needless diffidences, banishment of friends, dissipation of cohorts, nuptial breaches, and I know not what.

EDG.   How long have you been a sectary astronomical?[14]

---

11. *the surfeit*] the morbid excesses.

12. *pat he comes . . . old comedy*] In ancient comedies, the catastrophe was brought about in defiance of the natural order of things by the entry of a dominant character in quite unjustifiable circumstances.

13. *Tom o' Bedlam*] a generic name for mad beggars who often roamed the countryside; Bedlam refers to the London insane asylum at the Hospital of St. Mary of Bethlehem.

14. *a sectary astronomical*] a devotee of astronomy.

EDM.   Come, come; when saw you my father last?
EDG.   Why, the night gone by.
EDM.   Spake you with him?
EDG.   Ay, two hours together.
EDM.   Parted you in good terms? Found you no displeasure in him by
        word or countenance?
EDG.   None at all.
EDM.   Bethink yourself wherein you may have offended him: and at
        my entreaty forbear his presence till some little time hath qualified
        the heat of his displeasure, which at this instant so rageth in him
        that with the mischief of your person it would scarcely allay.
EDG.   Some villain hath done me wrong.
EDM.   That's my fear. I pray you, have a continent forbearance[15] till
        the speed of his rage goes slower, and, as I say, retire with me to my
        lodging, from whence I will fitly bring you to hear my lord speak:
        pray ye, go; there's my key: if you do stir abroad, go armed.
EDG.   Armed, brother!
EDM.   Brother, I advise you to the best: go armed: I am no honest
        man if there be any good meaning towards you: I have told you
        what I have seen and heard; but faintly, nothing like the image and
        horror of it: pray you, away.
EDG.   Shall I hear from you anon?
EDM.   I do serve you in this business.   [*Exit Edgar.*]
        A credulous father, and a brother noble,
        Whose nature is so far from doing harms
        That he suspects none; on whose foolish honesty
        My practices ride easy. I see the business.
        Let me, if not by birth, have lands by wit:
        All with me's meet that I can fashion fit.[16]   [*Exit.*]

---

15. *have a continent forbearance*] keep a well-controlled distance, a restrained aloofness,
    deliberately keep away (from him).
16. *All with me's meet . . . fit*] With me every device that I can adapt to my purpose is fair
    game.

SCENE III — *The Duke of Albany's Palace*

Enter GONERIL *and* OSWALD, *her steward*

GON.   Did my father strike my gentleman for chiding of his fool?

OSW.   Yes, madam.

GON.   By day and night he wrongs me; every hour
He flashes into one gross crime or other,
That sets us all at odds: I'll not endure it:
His knights grow riotous, and himself upbraids us
On every trifle. When he returns from hunting,
I will not speak with him; say I am sick:
If you come slack of[1] former services,
You shall do well; the fault of it I'll answer.

OSW.   He's coming, madam; I hear him.   [*Horns within.*]

GON.   Put on what weary negligence you please,
You and your fellows; I'ld have it come to question:
If he distaste it, let him to our sister,
Whose mind and mine, I know, in that are one,
Not to be over-ruled. Idle old man,
That still would manage those authorities
That he hath given away! Now, by my life,
Old fools are babes again, and must be used
With checks as flatteries, when they are seen abused.
Remember what I tell you.

OSW.   Very well, madam.

GON.   And let his knights have colder looks among you;
What grows of it, no matter; advise your fellows so:
I would breed from hence occasions, and I shall,
That I may speak: I'll write straight to my sister,
To hold my very course. Prepare for dinner.   [*Exeunt.*]

---

1. *come slack of*] be remiss in.

SCENE IV — *A Hall in the Same*

Enter KENT, *disguised*

KENT.   If but as well I other accents borrow,
         That can my speech defuse,[1] my good intent
         May carry through itself to that full issue
         For which I razed my likeness. Now, banish'd Kent,
         If thou canst serve where thou dost stand condemn'd,
         So may it come, thy master whom thou lovest
         Shall find thee full of labours.[2]

Horns within. Enter LEAR, Knights, *and* Attendants

LEAR.   Let me not stay a jot for dinner; go get it ready. [*Exit an Attendant.*] How now! what art thou?
KENT.   A man, sir.
LEAR.   What dost thou profess? What wouldst thou with us?
KENT.   I do profess to be no less than I seem; to serve him truly that will put me in trust; to love him that is honest; to converse with him that is wise and says little; to fear judgement; to fight when I cannot choose, and to eat no fish.[3]
LEAR.   What art thou?
KENT.   A very honest-hearted fellow, and as poor as the king.
LEAR.   If thou be as poor for a subject as he is for a king, thou art poor enough. What wouldst thou?
KENT.   Service.
LEAR.   Who wouldst thou serve?
KENT.   You.
LEAR.   Dost thou know me, fellow?

---

1. *defuse*] disorder, confuse. Kent is anxious to complete his disguise by adopting an accent which shall make his speech indistinct.
2. *full of labours*] ready for any service.
3. *to eat no fish*] Eating fish was held to be the sign of a Roman Catholic, of one disaffected to the government. Hence "to eat no fish" is equivalent to a profession of loyalty and orthodoxy.

KENT.   No, sir; but you have that in your countenance which I would
          fain call master.
LEAR.   What's that?
KENT.   Authority.
LEAR.   What services canst thou do?
KENT.   I can keep honest counsel, ride, run, mar a curious tale
          in telling it, and deliver a plain message bluntly: that which or-
          dinary men are fit for, I am qualified in, and the best of me is
          diligence.
LEAR.   How old art thou?
KENT.   Not so young, sir, to love a woman for singing, nor so old to
          dote on her for any thing: I have years on my back forty eight.
LEAR.   Follow me; thou shalt serve me: if I like thee no worse after
          dinner, I will not part from thee yet. Dinner, ho, dinner! Where's
          my knave? my fool? Go you, and call my fool hither.
                                                    [*Exit an Attendant.*]

Enter OSWALD

          You, you, sirrah, where's my daughter?
OSW.   So please you, —   [*Exit.*]
LEAR.   What says the fellow there? Call the clotpoll⁴ back. [*Exit a
          Knight.*] Where's my fool, ho? I think the world's asleep.

Re-enter Knight

          How now! where's that mongrel?
KNIGHT.   He says, my lord, your daughter is not well.
LEAR.   Why came not the slave back to me when I called him?
KNIGHT.   Sir, he answered me in the roundest⁵ manner, he would not.
LEAR.   He would not!
KNIGHT.   My lord, I know not what the matter is; but, to my judge-
          ment, your highness is not entertained with that ceremonious
          affection as you were wont; there's a great abatement of kindness
          appears as well in the general dependants as in the duke himself
          also and your daughter.
LEAR.   Ha! sayest thou so?

---

4. *clotpoll*] clodpate, blockhead.
5. *roundest*] bluntest.

KNIGHT.   I beseech you, pardon me, my lord, if I be mistaken; for my
duty cannot be silent when I think your highness wronged.

LEAR.   Thou but rememberest me of mine own conception: I have
perceived a most faint[6] neglect of late; which I have rather blamed
as mine own jealous curiosity than as a very pretence and purpose
of unkindness: I will look further into't. But where's my fool? I have
not seen him this two days.

KNIGHT.   Since my young lady's going into France, sir, the fool hath
much pined away.

LEAR.   No more of that; I have noted it well. Go you, and tell my
daughter I would speak with her. [*Exit an Attendant.*] Go you, call
hither my fool.   [*Exit an Attendant.*]

Re-enter OSWALD

O, you sir, you, come you hither, sir: who am I, sir?

OSW.   My lady's father.

LEAR.   My lady's father! my lord's knave: you whoreson dog! you
slave! you cur!

OSW.   I am none of these, my lord; I beseech your pardon.

LEAR.   Do you bandy looks with me, you rascal?   [*Striking him.*]

OSW.   I'll not be struck, my lord.

KENT.   Nor tripped neither, you base foot-ball player.

[*Tripping up his heels.*]

LEAR.   I thank thee, fellow; thou servest me, and I'll love thee.

KENT.   Come, sir, arise, away! I'll teach you differences:[7] away, away!
If you will measure your lubber's length again, tarry: but away! go
to; have you wisdom? so.   [*Pushes Oswald out.*]

LEAR.   Now, my friendly knave, I thank thee: there's earnest[8] of thy
service.   [*Giving Kent money.*]

Enter Fool

FOOL.   Let me hire him too: here's my coxcomb.[9]

[*Offering Kent his cap.*]

LEAR.   How now, my pretty knave! how dost thou?

---

6. *faint*] listless, languid.
7. *differences*] differences of rank.
8. *earnest*] earnest money, payment in advance.
9. *coxcomb*] the fool's cap.

FOOL.   Sirrah, you were best take my coxcomb.

KENT.   Why, fool?

FOOL.   Why, for taking one's part that's out of favour: nay, an thou
          canst not smile as the wind sits, thou'lt catch cold shortly: there,
          take my coxcomb: why, this fellow hath banished two on's daugh-
          ters, and done the third a blessing against his will; if thou follow
          him, thou must needs wear my coxcomb. How now, nuncle![10]
          Would I had two coxcombs and two daughters!

LEAR.   Why, my boy?

FOOL.   If I gave them all my living, I'ld keep my coxcombs myself.
          There's mine; beg another of thy daughters.

LEAR.   Take heed, sirrah; the whip.

FOOL.   Truth 's a dog must to kennel; he must be whipped out, when
          Lady the brach may stand by the fire and stink.

LEAR.   A pestilent gall to me!

FOOL.   Sirrah, I'll teach thee a speech.

LEAR.   Do.

FOOL.   Mark it, nuncle:

> Have more than thou showest,
> Speak less than thou knowest,
> Lend less than thou owest,[11]
> Ride more than thou goest,[12]
> Learn more than thou trowest,
> Set less than thou throwest;
> Leave thy drink and thy whore,
> And keep in-a-door,
> And thou shalt have more
> Than two tens to a score.

KENT.   This is nothing, fool.

FOOL.   Then 't is like the breath of an unfee'd lawyer, you gave me
          nothing for't. Can you make no use of nothing, nuncle?

LEAR.   Why, no, boy; nothing can be made out of nothing.

FOOL.   [To Kent] Prithee, tell him, so much the rent of his land comes
          to: he will not believe a fool.

---

10. *nuncle*] a contraction of "mine uncle." Fools usually addressed their superiors this way.
11. *owest*] ownest, possessest.
12. *goest*] walkest on foot.

LEAR.   A bitter fool!

FOOL.   Dost thou know the difference, my boy, between a bitter fool
and a sweet fool?

LEAR.   No, lad; teach me.

FOOL.

> That lord that counsell'd thee
>   To give away thy land,
> Come place him here by me;
>   Do thou for him stand:
> The sweet and bitter fool
>   Will presently appear;
> The one in motley[13] here,
>   The other found out there.

LEAR.   Dost thou call me fool, boy?

FOOL.   All thy other titles thou hast given away; that thou wast born
with.

KENT.   This is not altogether fool, my lord.

FOOL.   No, faith, lords and great men will not let me; if I had a
monopoly out,[14] they would have part on't: and ladies too, they will
not let me have all the fool to myself; they'll be snatching. Give me
an egg, nuncle, and I'll give thee two crowns.

LEAR.   What two crowns shall they be?

FOOL.   Why, after I have cut the egg in the middle and eat up the
meat, the two crowns of the egg. When thou clovest thy crown i' the
middle and gavest away both parts, thou borest thine ass on thy
back[15] o'er the dirt: thou hadst little wit in thy bald crown when
thou gavest thy golden one away. If I speak like myself[16] in this, let
him be whipped that first finds it so.

> [*Singing*]   Fools had ne'er less wit in a year;
>   For wise men are grown foppish,
> And know not how their wits to wear,
>   Their manners are so apish.

---

13. *motley*] the ordinary parti-coloured dress of the domestic fool.
14. *if I had a monopoly out*] in folly.
15. *borest thine ass . . . back*] An allusion to Æsop's fable of the old man who tried to please
everybody.
16. *like myself*] like a fool.

LEAR.   When were you wont to be so full of songs, sirrah?

FOOL.   I have used it, nuncle, ever since thou madest thy daughters
          thy mother: for when thou gavest them the rod and puttest down
          thine own breeches,

> [*Singing*]   Then they for sudden joy did weep,
>   And I for sorrow sung,
>   That such a king should play bo-peep,
>   And go the fools among.

Prithee, nuncle, keep a schoolmaster that can teach thy fool to lie: I
would fain learn to lie.

LEAR.   An you lie, sirrah, we'll have you whipped.

FOOL.   I marvel what kin thou and thy daughters are: they'll have me
          whipped for speaking true, thou'lt have me whipped for lying, and
          sometimes I am whipped for holding my peace. I had rather be any
          kind o' thing than a fool: and yet I would not be thee, nuncle; thou
          hast pared thy wit o' both sides and left nothing i' the middle. Here
          comes one o' the parings.

Enter GONERIL

LEAR.   How now, daughter! what makes that frontlet[17] on? Methinks
          you are too much of late i' the frown.

FOOL.   Thou wast a pretty fellow when thou hadst no need to care for
          her frowning; now thou art an O without a figure:[18] I am better
          than thou art now; I am a fool, thou art nothing. [*To Gon.*] Yes,
          forsooth, I will hold my tongue; so your face bids me, though you
          say nothing.

> Mum, mum:
> He that keeps nor crust nor crumb,
> Weary of all, shall want some.

[*Pointing to Lear*] That's a shealed peascod.[19]

GON.   Not only, sir, this your all-licensed fool,
          But other of your insolent retinue
          Do hourly carp and quarrel, breaking forth

---

17. *frontlet*] a tight band worn on women's foreheads, but here a frown.
18. *an O without a figure*] a cipher.
19. *a shealed peascod*] an empty husk, or pod without the peas; "shealed" is the old spelling
    of "shelled."

In rank and not to be endured riots. Sir,
I had thought, by making this well known unto you,
To have found a safe redress; but now grow fearful,
By what yourself too late have spoke and done,
That you protect this course and put it on
By your allowance; which if you should, the fault
Would not 'scape censure, nor the redresses sleep,
Which, in the tender of a wholesome weal,
Might in their working do you that offence
Which else were shame, that then necessity
Will call discreet proceeding.

FOOL.   For, you know, nuncle,

       The hedge-sparrow fed the cuckoo so long,
       That it had it head bit off by it young.[20]

So out went the candle, and we were left darkling.[21]

LEAR.   Are you our daughter?

GON.   Come, sir,
I would you would make use of that good wisdom,
Whereof I know you are fraught, and put away
These dispositions that of late transform you
From what you rightly are.

FOOL.   May not an ass know when the cart draws the horse? Whoop,
Jug! I love thee.[22]

LEAR.   Doth any here know me? This is not Lear:
Doth Lear walk thus? speak thus? Where are his eyes?
Either his notion weakens, his discernings
Are lethargied — Ha! waking? 't is not so.
Who is it that can tell me who I am?

FOOL.   Lear's shadow.

LEAR.   I would learn that; for, by the marks of sovereignty, knowledge
and reason, I should be false persuaded I had daughters.

---

20. *it head . . . it young*] in both cases "it" is the old form of "its." The lines refer to the
cuckoo's habit of laying her eggs in the sparrow's nest. The sparrow is wont to hatch and
nurture the cuckoo's chicks, though when they grow up they often kill the bird which
has cherished them.
21. *darkling*] in the dark.
22. *Whoop, Jug! I love thee*] Possibly the burden of an old song. "Jug" was the pet name for
Joan.

FOOL. Which they will make an obedient father.
LEAR. Your name, fair gentlewoman?
GON.   This admiration, sir, is much o' the savour
       Of other your new pranks. I do beseech you
       To understand my purposes aright:
       As you are old and reverend, you should be wise.
       Here do you keep a hundred knights and squires;
       Men so disorder'd, so debosh'd[23] and bold,
       That this our court, infected with their manners,
       Shows like a riotous inn: epicurism and lust
       Make it more like a tavern or a brothel
       Than a graced palace. The shame itself doth speak
       For instant remedy: be then desired
       By her that else will take the thing she begs
       A little to disquantity[24] your train,
       And the remainder that shall still depend,
       To be such men as may besort your age,
       Which know themselves and you.
LEAR.   Darkness and devils!
       Saddle my horses; call my train together.
       Degenerate bastard! I'll not trouble thee:
       Yet have I left a daughter.
GON.   You strike my people, and your disorder'd rabble
       Make servants of their betters.

Enter ALBANY

LEAR. Woe, that too late repents,— [*To Alb.*] O, sir, are you come?
       Is it your will? Speak, sir. Prepare my horses.
       Ingratitude, thou marble-hearted fiend,
       More hideous when thou show'st thee in a child
       Than the sea-monster![25]
ALB.   Pray, sir, be patient.
LEAR. [*To Gon.*] Detested kite! thou liest.
       My train are men of choice and rarest parts,
       That all particulars of duty know,

---

23. *debosh'd*] an old spelling of "debauched."
24. *disquantity*] diminish the quantity of.
25. *the sea-monster*] a vague reference to a sea-monster described in Ovid's *Metamorphoses*.

And in the most exact regard support
The worships[26] of their name. O most small fault,
How ugly didst thou in Cordelia show!
That, like an engine,[27] wrench'd my frame of nature
From the fix'd place, drew from my heart all love
And added to the gall. O Lear, Lear, Lear!
Beat at this gate, that let thy folly in [*Striking his head.*]
And thy dear judgement out! Go, go, my people.

ALB.   My lord, I am guiltless, as I am ignorant
Of what hath moved you.

LEAR.   It may be so, my lord.
Hear, nature, hear; dear goddess, hear!
Suspend thy purpose, if thou didst intend
To make this creature fruitful:
Into her womb convey sterility:
Dry up in her the organs of increase,
And from her derogate[28] body never spring
A babe to honour her! If she must teem,
Create her child of spleen, that it may live
And be a thwart disnatured torment to her.
Let it stamp wrinkles in her brow of youth;
With cadent[29] tears fret channels in her cheeks;
Turn all her mother's pains and benefits
To laughter and contempt; that she may feel
How sharper than a serpent's tooth it is
To have a thankless child! Away, away!   [*Exit.*]

ALB.   Now, gods that we adore, whereof comes this?

GON.   Never afflict yourself to know the cause,
But let his disposition have that scope
That dotage gives it.

Re-enter LEAR

LEAR.   What, fifty of my followers at a clap!
Within a fortnight!

ALB.   What's the matter, sir?

---

26. *The worships*] The honourable repute.
27. *like an engine*] like the rack.
28. *derogate*] degenerate or degraded.
29. *cadent*] falling.

LEAR.   I'll tell thee. [*To Gon.*] Life and death! I am ashamed
          That thou hast power to shake my manhood thus;
          That these hot tears, which break from me perforce,
          Should make thee worth them. Blasts and fogs upon thee!
          The untented[30] woundings of a father's curse
          Pierce every sense about thee! Old fond eyes,
          Beweep this cause again, I'll pluck ye out
          And cast you with the waters that you lose
          To temper clay. Yea, is it come to this?
          Let it be so: yet have I left a daughter,
          Who, I am sure, is kind and comfortable:
          When she shall hear this of thee, with her nails
          She'll flay thy wolvish visage. Thou shalt find
          That I'll resume the shape which thou dost think
          I have cast off for ever: thou shalt, I warrant thee.
                              [*Exeunt Lear, Kent, and Attendants.*]
GON.   Do you mark that, my lord?
ALB.   I cannot be so partial, Goneril,
          To the great love I bear you, —
GON.   Pray you, content. What, Oswald, ho!
          [*To the Fool*] You, sir, more knave than fool, after your master.
FOOL.   Nuncle Lear, nuncle Lear, tarry; take the fool with thee.

                    A fox, when one has caught her,
                    And such a daughter,
                    Should sure to the slaughter,
                    If my cap would buy a halter:
                    So the fool follows after.   [*Exit.*]

GON.   This man hath had good counsel: a hundred knights!
          'T is politic and safe to let him keep
          At point[31] a hundred knights: yes, that on every dream,
          Each buzz, each fancy, each complaint, dislike,
          He may enguard his dotage with their powers
          And hold our lives in mercy. Oswald, I say!
ALB.   Well, you may fear too far.
GON.   Safer than trust too far:

---

30. *untented*] not to be healed, incapable of yielding to the surgeon's healing "tent" or
    probe.
31. *At point*] Equipped.

Let me still take away the harms I fear,
Not fear still to be taken: I know his heart.
What he hath utter'd I have writ my sister:
If she sustain him and his hundred knights,
When I have show'd the unfitness,—

Re-enter OSWALD

                                                    How now, Oswald!
          What, have you writ that letter to my sister?
OSW.   Yes, madam.
GON.   Take you some company, and away to horse
          Inform her full of my particular fear,
          And thereto add such reasons of your own
          As may compact it more.[32] Get you gone;
          And hasten your return. [*Exit Oswald.*] No, no, my lord,
          This milky gentleness and course of yours
          Though I condemn not, yet, under pardon,
          You are much more attask'd[33] for want of wisdom
          Than praised for harmful mildness.
ALB.   How far your eyes may pierce I cannot tell:
          Striving to better, oft we mar what's well.
GON.   Nay, then—
ALB.   Well, well; the event.[34]   [*Exeunt.*]

---

32. *compact it more*] strengthen it.
33. *attask'd*] (to be) taken to task, reproved.
34. *the event*] (we'll wait to see) how it turns out.

SCENE V — *Court Before the Same*

Enter LEAR, KENT, *and* Fool

LEAR.   Go you before to Gloucester with these letters. Acquaint my
daughter no further with any thing you know than comes from her
demand out of the letter. If your diligence be not speedy, I shall be
there afore you.

KENT.   I will not sleep, my lord, till I have delivered your letter.

[Exit.]

FOOL.   If a man's brains were in 's heels, were't not in danger of
kibes?[1]

LEAR.   Ay, boy.

FOOL.   Then, I prithee, be merry; thy wit shall ne'er go slip-shod.[2]

LEAR.   Ha, ha, ha!

FOOL.   Shalt see thy other daughter will use thee kindly; for though
she's as like this as a crab 's like an apple, yet I can tell what I can
tell.

LEAR.   Why, what canst thou tell, my boy?

FOOL.   She will taste as like this as a crab[3] does to a crab. Thou canst
tell why one's nose stands i' the middle on 's face?

LEAR.   No.

FOOL.   Why, to keep one's eyes of either side 's nose, that what a man
cannot smell out he may spy into.

LEAR.   I did her[4] wrong —

FOOL.   Canst tell how an oyster makes his shell?

LEAR.   No.

FOOL.   Nor I neither; but I can tell why a snail has a house.

LEAR.   Why?

FOOL.   Why, to put's head in; not to give it away to his daughters, and
leave his horns without a case.

---

1. *kibes*] chilblains.
2. *thy wit . . . slip-shod*] "slipshod" means "in slippers," the natural footgear for sore heels.
The Fool means that Lear has no brains, and thus will never need slippers.
3. *crab*] crabapple.
4. *her*] Cordelia.

LEAR.   I will forget my nature. — So kind a father! — Be my horses
ready?
FOOL.   Thy asses are gone about 'em. The reason why the seven stars
are no more than seven is a pretty reason.
LEAR.   Because they are not eight?
FOOL.   Yes, indeed: thou wouldst make a good fool.
LEAR.   To take 't again perforce![5] Monster ingratitude!
FOOL.   If thou wert my fool, nuncle, I'ld have thee beaten for being
old before thy time.
LEAR.   How's that?
FOOL.   Thou shouldst not have been old till thou hadst been wise.
LEAR.   O, let me not be mad, not mad, sweet heaven!
Keep me in temper: I would not be mad!

Enter Gentleman

How now! are the horses ready?
GENT.   Ready, my lord.
LEAR.   Come, boy.
FOOL.   She that's a maid now and laughs at my departure
Shall not be a maid long, unless things be cut shorter.
                                                    [*Exeunt.*]

---

5. *To take 't again perforce*] No doubt Lear is meditating a forcible resumption of his royal
power.

ACT II

SCENE I — *The Earl of Gloucester's Castle*

Enter EDMUND *and* CURAN, *meeting*

EDM.   Save thee, Curan.

CUR.   And you, sir. I have been with your father, and given him notice that the Duke of Cornwall and Regan his duchess will be here with him this night.

EDM.   How comes that?

CUR.   Nay, I know not. You have heard of the news abroad, I mean the whispered ones, for they are yet but ear-kissing arguments?[1]

EDM.   Not I: pray you, what are they?

CUR.   Have you heard of no likely wars toward, 'twixt the Dukes of Cornwall and Albany?

EDM.   Not a word.

CUR.   You may do then in time. Fare you well, sir.

[*Exit.*]

EDM.   The duke be here to-night? The better! best!
　　　　　This weaves itself perforce into my business.
　　　　　My father hath set guard to take my brother;
　　　　　And I have one thing, of a queasy question,[2]
　　　　　Which I must act: briefness and fortune, work!
　　　　　Brother, a word; descend: brother, I say!

Enter EDGAR

---

1. *ear-kissing arguments*] expressions that lightly touch the ear, topics merely spoken of in an undertone.
2. *of a queasy question*] of a delicate or ticklish character.

My father watches: O sir, fly this place;
Intelligence is given where you are hid;
You have now the good advantage of the night:
Have you not spoken 'gainst the Duke of Cornwall?
He's coming hither, now, i' the night, i' the haste,
And Regan with him: have you nothing said
Upon his party 'gainst the Duke of Albany?
Advise yourself.

EDG.   I am sure on't, not a word.

EDM.   I hear my father coming: pardon me:
In cunning I must draw my sword upon you:[3]
Draw: seem to defend yourself: now quit you well.
Yield: come before my father. Light, ho, here!
Fly, brother. Torches, torches! So farewell.

                              [*Exit Edgar.*]

Some blood drawn on me would beget opinion[4]

                              [*Wounds his arm.*]

Of my more fierce endeavour: I have seen drunkards
Do more than this in sport. Father, father!
Stop, stop! No help?

Enter GLOUCESTER, *and* Servants *with torches*

GLOU.   Now, Edmund, where's the villain?

EDM.   Here stood he in the dark, his sharp sword out,
Mumbling of wicked charms, conjuring the moon
To stand's auspicious mistress.

GLOU.   But where is he?

EDM.   Look, sir, I bleed.

GLOU.   Where is the villain, Edmund?

EDM.   Fled this way, sir. When by no means he could —

GLOU.   Pursue him, ho! — Go after. [*Exeunt some Servants.*] "By no
means" what?

EDM.   Persuade me to the murder of your lordship;
But that I told him the revenging gods
'Gainst parricides did all their thunders bend,
Spoke with how manifold and strong a bond

---

3. *In cunning . . . you*] I must pretend to draw my sword on you.
4. *beget opinion*] create the illusion.

The child was bound to the father; sir, in fine,
Seeing how loathly opposite I stood
To his unnatural purpose, in fell motion
With his prepared sword he charges home
My unprovided body, lanced mine arm:
But when he saw my best alarum'd spirits[5]
Bold in the quarrel's right, roused to the encounter,
Or whether gasted by[6] the noise I made,
Full suddenly he fled.

GLOU.   Let him fly far:
Not in this land shall he remain uncaught;
And found — dispatch.[7] The noble duke my master,
My worthy arch and patron, comes to-night:
By his authority I will proclaim it,
That he which finds him shall deserve our thanks,
Bringing the murderous caitiff[8] to the stake;
He that conceals him, death.

EDM.   When I dissuaded him from his intent
And found him pight[9] to do it, with curst speech
I threaten'd to discover him: he replied,
"Thou unpossessing bastard! dost thou think,
If I would stand against thee, could the reposure[10]
Of any trust, virtue, or worth, in thee
Make thy words faith'd? No: what I should deny —
As this I would; ay, though thou didst produce
My very character — I'ld turn it all
To thy suggestion, plot, and damned practice:
And thou must make a dullard of the world,
If they not thought the profits of my death
Were very pregnant and potential spurs
To make thee seek it."

GLOU.   Strong and fasten'd villain!

---

5. *my best alarum'd spirits*] my finest courage roused to action.
6. *gasted by*] frightened by, aghast at.
7. *And found — dispatch*] An elliptical expression for "and when he is *found* there shall be no delay; he shall be killed outright."
8. *caitiff*] wretch.
9. *pight*] settled or pledged.
10. *reposure*] the act of ascribing, attributing.

Would he deny his letter? I never got[11] him.

[*Tucket within.*]

Hark, the duke's trumpets! I know not why he comes.
All ports I'll bar; the villain shall not 'scape;
The duke must grant me that: besides, his picture
I will send far and near, that all the kingdom
May have due note of him; and of my land,
Loyal and natural boy, I'll work the means
To make thee capable.[12]

Enter CORNWALL, REGAN, *and* Attendants

CORN. How now, my noble friend! since I came hither,
       Which I can call but now, I have heard strange news.
REG.   If it be true, all vengeance comes too short
       Which can pursue the offender. How dost, my lord?
GLOU. O, madam, my old heart is crack'd, is crack'd!
REG.   What, did my father's godson seek your life?
       He whom my father named? your Edgar?
GLOU. O, lady, lady, shame would have it hid!
REG.   Was he not companion with the riotous knights
       That tend upon my father?
GLOU. I know not, madam: 't is too bad, too bad.
EDM.   Yes, madam, he was of that consort.
REG.   No marvel then, though he were ill affected:
       'T is they have put him on the old man's death,
       To have the waste and spoil of his revenues.
       I have this present evening from my sister
       Been well inform'd of them, and with such cautions
       That if they come to sojourn at my house,
       I'll not be there.
CORN.   Nor I, assure thee, Regan.
       Edmund, I hear that you have shown your father
       A child-like office.
EDM.   'T was my duty, sir.
GLOU. He did bewray his practice,[13] and received
       This hurt you see, striving to apprehend him.

---

11. *got*] begot.
12. *I'll work . . . capable*] I'll make sure you fall heir to (my land).
13. *bewray his practice*] betray his (Edgar's) plot.

CORN. Is he pursued?
GLOU.   Ay, my good lord.
CORN. If he be taken, he shall never more
Be fear'd of doing harm: make your own purpose,
How in my strength you please. For you, Edmund,
Whose virtue and obedience doth this instant
So much commend itself, you shall be ours:
Natures of such deep trust we shall much need:
You we first seize on.
EDM.   I shall serve you, sir,
Truly, however else.
GLOU.   For him I thank your grace.
CORN. You know not why we came to visit you, —
REG. Thus out of season, threading dark-eyed night:
Occasions, noble Gloucester, of some poise,[14]
Wherein we must have use of your advice:
Our father he hath writ, so hath our sister,
Of differences, which I least thought it fit
To answer from our home; the several messengers
From hence attend dispatch.[15] Our good old friend,
Lay comforts to your bosom, and bestow
Your needful counsel to our business,
Which craves the instant use.
GLOU.   I serve you, madam:
Your graces are right welcome.   [*Flourish. Exeunt.*]

---

14. *poise*] weight, importance.
15. *attend dispatch*] wait to be dispatched.

SCENE II — *Before Gloucester's Castle*

Enter KENT *and* OSWALD, *severally*

OSW.   Good dawning[1] to thee, friend: art of this house?
KENT.   Ay.
OSW.   Where may we set our horses?
KENT.   I' the mire.
OSW.   Prithee, if thou lovest me, tell me.
KENT.   I love thee not.
OSW.   Why then I care not for thee.
KENT.   If I had thee in Lipsbury pinfold,[2] I would make thee care for
    me.
OSW.   Why dost thou use me thus? I know thee not.
KENT.   Fellow, I know thee.
OSW.   What dost thou know me for?
KENT.   A knave; a rascal; an eater of broken meats; a base, proud,
    shallow, beggarly, three-suited, hundred-pound, filthy, worsted-
    stocking[3] knave; a lily-livered action-taking knave; a whoreson,
    glass-gazing, superserviceable,[4] finical rogue; one-trunk-
    inheriting[5] slave; one that wouldst be a bawd in way of good
    service, and art nothing but the composition of a knave, beggar,
    coward, pandar, and the son and heir of a mongrel bitch: one
    whom I will beat into clamorous whining, if thou deniest the least
    syllable of thy addition.[6]

---

1. *dawning*] the time about daybreak.
2. *Lipsbury pinfold*] "Pinfold" is a synonym for "pound," a public enclosure for the confine-
    ment of stray cattle. Lipsbury is unexplained. It is perhaps a coined word sarcastically
    meaning "the lips." Kent might be threatening to get Oswald between his teeth.
3. *worsted-stocking*] Poor people wore worsted stockings, while the stockings of rich people
    were invariably of silk.
4. *action-taking knave*] one who resorts to legal action when assaulted instead of challeng-
    ing an assailant to fight.
    glass-gazing] surveying his person in a looking-glass.
    superserviceable] one above his duties.
5. *one-trunk-inheriting*] possessing a stock of clothes which would all go into a single trunk.
6. *addition*] title.

Osw.   Why, what a monstrous fellow art thou, thus to rail on one that
          is neither known of thee nor knows thee!
KENT.   What a brazen-faced varlet art thou, to deny thou knowest me!
          Is it two days ago since I tripped up thy heels and beat thee before
          the king? Draw, you rogue: for, though it be night, yet the moon
          shines; I'll make a sop o' the moonshine of you: draw, you whore-
          son cullionly barber-monger,[7] draw.   [*Drawing his sword.*]
Osw.   Away! I have nothing to do with thee.
KENT.   Draw, you rascal: you come with letters against the king, and
          take vanity the puppet's part against the royalty of her father: draw,
          you rogue, or I'll so carbonado[8] your shanks: draw, you rascal;
          come your ways.
Osw.   Help, ho! murder! help!
KENT.   Strike, you slave; stand, rogue; stand, you neat slave, strike.
                                                              [*Beating him.*]
Osw.   Help, ho! murder! murder!

Enter EDMUND, *with his rapier drawn*, CORNWALL, REGAN, GLOUCES-
TER, *and* Servants

EDM.   How now! What's the matter?   [*Parting them.*]
KENT.   With you, goodman boy, an you please: come, I'll flesh you;
          come on, young master.
GLOU.   Weapons! arms! What's the matter here?
CORN.   Keep peace, upon your lives;
          He dies that strikes again. What is the matter?
REG.   The messengers from our sister and the king.
CORN.   What is your difference? speak.
Osw.   I am scarce in breath, my lord.
KENT.   No marvel, you have so bestirred your valour. You cowardly
          rascal, nature disclaims in thee: a tailor made thee.
CORN.   Thou art a strange fellow: a tailor make a man?
KENT.   Ay, a tailor, sir: a stone-cutter or a painter could not have made
          him so ill, though he had been but two hours at the trade.
CORN.   Speak yet, how grew your quarrel?

---

7. *cullionly barber-monger*] rascally frequenter of barbers' shops, who was forever getting his
   hair and beard trimmed.
8. *carbonado*] slash; a culinary term.

OSW.   This ancient ruffian, sir, whose life I have spared at suit of his
         gray beard, —
KENT.   Thou whoreson zed! thou unnecessary letter![9] My lord, if you
         will give me leave, I will tread this unbolted villain into mortar, and
         daub the walls of a jakes[10] with him. Spare my gray beard, you
         wagtail?
CORN.   Peace, sirrah!
         You beastly knave, know you no reverence?
KENT.   Yes, sir; but anger hath a privilege.
CORN.   Why art thou angry?
KENT.   That such a slave as this should wear a sword,
         Who wears no honesty. Such smiling rogues as these,
         Like rats, oft bite the holy cords[11] a-twain
         Which are too intrinse[12] to unloose; smooth every passion
         That in the natures of their lords rebel;
         Bring oil to fire, snow to their colder moods;
         Renege, affirm, and turn their halcyon[13] beaks
         With every gale and vary of their masters,
         Knowing nought, like dogs, but following.
         A plague upon your epileptic visage!
         Smile you my speeches, as I were a fool?
         Goose, if I had you upon Sarum[14] plain,
         I'ld drive ye cackling home to Camelot.
CORN.   What, art thou mad, old fellow?
GLOU.   How fell you out? say that.
KENT.   No contraries hold more antipathy
         Than I and such a knave.
CORN.   Why dost thou call him knave? What is his fault?
KENT.   His countenance likes me not.

---

 9. *zed . . . letter*] According to Ben Jonson's *English Grammar*, "Zed is a letter often heard
    among us, but seldom seen."
10. *a jakes*] an outhouse or privy.
11. *holy cords*] bonds of filial affection.
12. *intrinse*] tightly knotted.
13. *halcyon*] the kingfisher. There was a popular belief that if the bird was suspended in the
    air by a cord round its neck, its bill would always point to the quarter from which the
    wind blew.
14. *Sarum*] Salisbury.

CORN.   No more perchance does mine, nor his, nor hers.
KENT.   Sir, 't is my occupation to be plain:
           I have seen better faces in my time
           Than stands on any shoulder that I see
           Before me at this instant.
CORN.   This is some fellow,
           Who, having been praised for bluntness, doth affect
           A saucy roughness, and constrains the garb
           Quite from his nature:[15] he cannot flatter, he, —
           An honest mind and plain, — he must speak truth
           An they will take it, so; if not, he's plain.
           These kind of knaves I know, which in this plainness
           Harbour more craft and more corrupter ends
           Than twenty silly ducking observants
           That stretch their duties nicely.
KENT.   Sir, in good faith, in sincere verity,
           Under the allowance of your great aspect,
           Whose influence, like the wreath of radiant fire
           On flickering Phoebus' front, —
CORN.   What mean'st by this?
KENT.   To go out of my dialect, which you discommend so much. I
      know, sir, I am no flatterer: he that beguiled you in a plain accent
      was a plain knave; which, for my part, I will not be, though I should
      win your displeasure to entreat me to 't.
CORN.   What was the offence you gave him?
OSW.   I never gave him any:
           It pleased the king his master very late
           To strike at me, upon his misconstruction;[16]
           When he, conjunct,[17] and flattering his displeasure,
           Tripp'd me behind; being down, insulted, rail'd,
           And put upon him such a deal of man,
           That worthied him, got praises of the king
           For him attempting who was self-subdued,

---

15. *constrains . . . nature*] his frankness conceals a deceitful nature.
16. *misconstruction*] misapprehension.
17. *conjunct*] in concert or alliance (with Lear).

And in the fleshment[18] of this dread exploit
Drew on me here again.

KENT.   None of these rogues and cowards
But Ajax[19] is their fool.

CORN.   Fetch forth the stocks!
You stubborn ancient knave, you reverend braggart,
We'll teach you—

KENT.   Sir, I am too old to learn:
Call not your stocks for me: I serve the king,
On whose employment I was sent to you:
You shall do small respect, show too bold malice
Against the grace and person of my master,
Stocking his messenger.

CORN.   Fetch forth the stocks! As I have life and honour,
There shall he sit till noon.

REG.   Till noon! till night, my lord, and all night too.

KENT.   Why, madam, if I were your father's dog,
You should not use me so.

REG.   Sir, being his knave, I will.

CORN.   This is a fellow of the self-same colour
Our sister speaks of. Come, bring away the stocks!
                                    [*Stocks brought out.*]

GLOU.   Let me beseech your grace not to do so:
His fault is much, and the good king his master
Will check him for 't: your purposed low correction
Is such as basest and contemned'st wretches
For pilferings and most common trespasses
Are punish'd with: the king must take it ill,
That he, so slightly valued in his messenger,
Should have him thus restrain'd.

CORN.   I'll answer that.

REG.   My sister may receive it much more worse,
To have her gentleman abused, assaulted,
For following her affairs. Put in his legs.
                                    [*Kent is put in the stocks.*]

---

18. *fleshment*] insolence, fierceness.
19. *Ajax*] a synonym for a brave, blunt man, whom designing villains always make their butt
   or get the better of.

                Come, my good lord, away.
                                    [Exeunt all but Gloucester and Kent.]
GLOU.   I am sorry for thee, friend; 't is the duke's pleasure,
            Whose disposition, all the world well knows,
            Will not be rubb'd[20] nor stopp'd: I'll entreat for thee.
KENT.   Pray, do not, sir: I have watch'd and travell'd hard;
            Some time I shall sleep out, the rest I'll whistle.
            A good man's fortune may grow out at heels:
            Give you good morrow!
GLOU.   The duke's to blame in this; 't will be ill taken.   *[Exit.]*
KENT.   Good king, that must approve the common saw,
            Thou out of heaven's benediction comest
            To the warm sun![21]
            Approach, thou beacon to this under globe,
            That by thy comfortable beams I may
            Peruse this letter! Nothing almost sees miracles
            But misery.[22] I know 't is from Cordelia,
            Who hath most fortunately been inform'd
            Of my obscured course; and shall find time
            From this enormous state, seeking to give
            Losses their remedies. All weary and o'er-watch'd,
            Take vantage, heavy eyes, not to behold
            This shameful lodging.
            Fortune, good night: smile once more; turn thy wheel!
                                                            [Sleeps.]

---

20. *rubb'd*] impeded, hindered.
21. *must approve . . . sun*] must make good the common proverb ("saw"), which says "out of
    God's blessing into the warm sun," meaning from a better to a worse place.
22. *Nothing . . . misery*] It is almost only by the unfortunate that miracles are looked for or
    seen; prosperous people stand in no need of them.

Scene III — A *Wood*

Enter Edgar

EDG.   I heard myself proclaim'd;
       And by the happy hollow of a tree
       Escaped the hunt. No port is free; no place,
       That guard and most unusual vigilance
       Does not attend my taking. Whiles I may 'scape
       I will preserve myself: and am bethought
       To take the basest and most poorest shape
       That ever penury in contempt of man
       Brought near to beast: my face I'll grime with filth,
       Blanket my loins, elf all my hair in knots,
       And with presented nakedness out-face
       The winds and persecutions of the sky.
       The country gives me proof and precedent
       Of Bedlam beggars,[1] who with roaring voices
       Strike in their numb'd and mortified bare arms
       Pins, wooden pricks,[2] nails, sprigs of rosemary;
       And with this horrible object,[3] from low farms,
       Poor pelting[4] villages, sheep-cotes and mills,
       Sometime with lunatic bans,[5] sometime with prayers,
       Enforce their charity. Poor Turlygod![6] poor Tom!
       That's something yet: Edgar I nothing am.[7]   [*Exit.*]

---

1. *Bedlam beggars*] half-crazy beggars, strictly applied to mendicant patients discharged from Bethlehem or Bedlam hospital, but often generally applied to pauper idiots.
2. *wooden pricks*] skewers of wood.
3. *object*] appearance.
4. *pelting*] paltry, contemptible.
5. *lunatic bans*] mad imprecations.
6. *Turlygod*] Perhaps a reference to a strange fraternity of naked beggars, which infested the continent of Europe in the fourteenth century, known as Turlupins; Turlygod has been doubtfully interpreted as a corrupted form of Turlupins.
7. *Edgar I nothing am*] I am no longer likely to be mistaken for Edgar. I have rid myself of his likeness.

SCENE IV — *Before Gloucester's Castle*

Kent in the Stocks

Enter LEAR, FOOL, *and* Gentleman

LEAR.   'T is strange that they should so depart from home,
        And not send back my messenger.
GENT.   As I learn'd,
        The night before there was no purpose in them
        Of this remove.
KENT.   Hail to thee, noble master!
LEAR.   Ha!
        Makest thou this shame thy pastime?
KENT.   No, my lord.
FOOL.   Ha, ha! he wears cruel garters. Horses are tied by the heads,
        dogs and bears by the neck, monkeys by the loins, and men by the
        legs: when a man's over-lusty at legs, then he wears wooden nether-
        stocks.[1]
LEAR.   What's he that hath so much thy place mistook
        To set thee here?
KENT.   It is both he and she;
        Your son and daughter.
LEAR.   No.
KENT.   Yes.
LEAR.   No, I say.
KENT.   I say, yea.
LEAR.   No, no, they would not.
KENT.   Yes, they have.
LEAR.   By Jupiter, I swear, no.
KENT.   By Juno, I swear, ay.
LEAR.   They durst not do't;
        They could not, would not do't; 't is worse than murder,

---

1. *nether-stocks*] stockings or socks, as opposed to knee breeches, the upper-stocks.

To do upon respect[2] such violent outrage:
Resolve me with all modest haste[3] which way
Thou mightst deserve, or they impose, this usage,
Coming from us.

KENT.   My lord, when at their home
I did commend your highness' letters to them,
Ere I was risen from the place that show'd
My duty kneeling, came there a reeking post,
Stew'd in his haste, half breathless, panting forth
From Goneril his mistress salutations;
Deliver'd letters, spite of intermission,[4]
Which presently they read: on whose contents
They summon'd up their meiny,[5] straight took horse;
Commanded me to follow and attend
The leisure of their answer; gave me cold looks:
And meeting here the other messenger,
Whose welcome, I perceived, had poison'd mine —
Being the very fellow that of late
Display'd so saucily against your highness —
Having more man than wit about me, drew:
He raised the house with loud and coward cries.
Your son and daughter found this trespass worth
The shame which here it suffers.

FOOL.   Winter's not gone yet, if the wild geese fly that way.

> Fathers that wear rags
>   Do make their children blind;
> But fathers that bear bags
>   Shall see their children kind.
> Fortune, that arrant whore,
> Ne'er turns the key[6] to the poor.

But, for all this, thou shalt have as many dolours[7] for thy
daughters as thou canst tell in a year.

---

2. *upon respect*] with deliberation.
3. *Resolve me . . . haste*] Inform me with all the speed that becomes a truthful statement.
4. *spite of intermission*] without any delay, at the cost of postponing my audience with them.
5. *meiny*] retinue, household.
6. *turns the key*] offers the key of her favours.
7. *dolours*] a pun on the word in the sense of the coin, and of grief.

LEAR.   O, how this mother[8] swells up toward my heart!
          Hysterica passio, down, thou climbing sorrow,
          Thy element's below! Where is this daughter?
KENT.   With the earl, sir, here within.
LEAR.   Follow me not; stay here.   [*Exit.*]
GENT.   Made you no more offence but what you speak of?
KENT.   None.
          How chance the king comes with so small a train?
FOOL.   An thou hadst been set i' the stocks for that question, thou
          hadst well deserved it.
KENT.   Why, fool?
FOOL.   We'll set thee to school to an ant, to teach thee there's no
          labouring i' the winter.[9] All that follow their noses are led by their
          eyes but blind men; and there's not a nose among twenty but can
          smell him that's stinking. Let go thy hold when a great wheel runs
          down a hill, lest it break thy neck with following it; but the great
          one that goes up the hill, let him draw thee after. When a wise man
          gives thee better counsel, give me mine again: I would have none
          but knaves follow it, since a fool gives it.

                    That sir which serves and seeks for gain,
                         And follows but for form,
                    Will pack when it begins to rain,
                         And leave thee in the storm.
                    But I will tarry; the fool will stay,
                         And let the wise man fly:
                    The knave turns fool that runs away;
                         The fool no knave, perdy.

KENT.   Where learned you this, fool?
FOOL.   Not i' the stocks, fool.

Re-enter LEAR, *with* GLOUCESTER

LEAR.   Deny to speak with me? They are sick? they are weary?
          They have travell'd all the night? Mere fetches;

---

8. *this mother*] the popular name of an hysterical malady, the chief symptom of which was a
   choking sensation in the throat. The disease was technically known as "hysterica passio."
9. *We'll set thee . . . winter*] A reference to Proverbs 6:6–8: "Go to the ant, thou sluggard;
   consider her ways, and be wise: which having no guide, overseer, or ruler, provideth her
   meat in the summer, and gathereth her food in the harvest."

        The images of revolt and flying off.[10]
        Fetch me a better answer.

GLOU.   My dear lord,
        You know the fiery quality of the duke;
        How unremoveable and fix'd he is
        In his own course.

LEAR.   Vengeance! plague! death! confusion!
        Fiery? what quality? Why, Gloucester, Gloucester,
        I'ld speak with the Duke of Cornwall and his wife.

GLOU.   Well, my good lord, I have inform'd them so.

LEAR.   Inform'd them! Dost thou understand me, man?

GLOU.   Ay, my good lord.

LEAR.   The king would speak with Cornwall; the dear father
        Would with his daughter speak, commands her service:
        Are they inform'd of this? My breath and blood!
        "Fiery"? "the fiery duke"? Tell the hot duke that —
        No, but not yet: may be he is not well:
        Infirmity doth still neglect all office
        Whereto our health is bound; we are not ourselves
        When nature being oppress'd commands the mind
        To suffer with the body: I'll forbear;
        And am fall'n out with my more headier will,
        To take the indisposed and sickly fit
        For the sound man. [*Looking on Kent*] Death on my state!
           wherefore
        Should he sit here? This act persuades me
        That this remotion[11] of the duke and her
        Is practice only. Give me my servant forth.
        Go tell the duke and's wife I'ld speak with them,
        Now, presently: bid them come forth and hear me,
        Or at their chamber-door I'll beat the drum
        Till it cry sleep to death.

GLOU.   I would have all well betwixt you.   [*Exit.*]

LEAR.   O me, my heart, my rising heart! But down!

---

10. *fetches ... flying off*] tricks or subterfuges; the tokens of rebellion and disaffection.
11. *remotion*] removal.

FOOL.   Cry to it, nuncle, as the cockney[12] did to the eels when she put
'em i' the paste alive; she knapped[13] 'em o' the coxcombs with a
stick, and cried "Down, wantons, down!" 'T was her brother that, in
pure kindness to his horse, buttered his hay.[14]

Re-enter GLOUCESTER, *with* CORNWALL, REGAN, *and* Servants

LEAR.   Good morrow to you both.
CORN.   Hail to your grace!
                                              [*Kent is set at liberty.*]
REG.   I am glad to see your highness.
LEAR.   Regan, I think you are; I know what reason
          I have to think so: if thou shouldst not be glad,
          I would divorce me from thy mother's tomb,
          Sepulchring an adultress. [*To Kent*] O, are you free?
          Some other time for that. Beloved Regan,
          Thy sister's naught: O Regan, she hath tied
          Sharp-tooth'd unkindness, like a vulture, here:
                                              [*Points to his heart.*]
          I can scarce speak to thee; thou'lt not believe
          With how depraved a quality — O Regan!
REG.   I pray you, sir, take patience: I have hope
          You less know how to value her desert
          Than she to scant her duty.
LEAR.   Say, how is that?
REG.   I cannot think my sister in the least
          Would fail her obligation: if, sir, perchance
          She have restrain'd the riots of your followers,
          'T is on such ground and to such wholesome end
          As clears her from all blame.
LEAR.   My curses on her!
REG.   O, sir, you are old;
          Nature in you stands on the very verge

───────────────

12. *cockney*] here used in the rare sense of a female "cook" or "scullion." It is more often
    applied to an effeminate man or woman.
13. *knapped*] cracked.
14. *buttered his hay*] a reference to the practice of dishonest ostlers, who sold for their own
    profit greased hay which the horses refused.

Of her confine: you should be ruled and led
By some discretion that discerns your state
Better than you yourself. Therefore I pray you
That to our sister you do make return;
Say you have wrong'd her, sir.

LEAR.   Ask her forgiveness?
Do you but mark how this becomes the house:[15]
[*Kneeling*] "Dear daughter, I confess that I am old;
Age is unnecessary: on my knees I beg
That you'll vouchsafe me raiment, bed and food."

REG.   Good sir, no more; these are unsightly tricks:
Return you to my sister.

LEAR.   [*Rising*]   Never, Regan:
She hath abated me of half my train;
Look'd black upon me; struck me with her tongue,
Most serpent-like, upon the very heart:
All the stored vengeances of heaven fall
On her ingrateful top! Strike her young bones,[16]
You taking airs,[17] with lameness.

CORN.   Fie, sir, fie!

LEAR.   You nimble lightnings, dart your blinding flames
Into her scornful eyes. Infect her beauty,
You fen-suck'd fogs, drawn by the powerful sun
To fall and blast her pride.

REG.   O the blest gods! so will you wish on me,
When the rash mood is on.

LEAR.   No, Regan, thou shalt never have my curse:
Thy tender-hefted[18] nature shall not give
Thee o'er to harshness: her eyes are fierce, but thine
Do comfort and not burn. 'T is not in thee
To grudge my pleasures, to cut off my train,
To bandy hasty words, to scant my sizes,[19]

---

15. *becomes the house*] fits family relations, suits the domestic ties between father and daughter.
16. *young bones*] unborn infants.
17. *taking airs*] airs that bewitch, strike with disease.
18. *tender-hefted*] Perhaps *tender-hefted* here means "of tender disposition."
19. *scant my sizes*] contract my allowances.

       And in conclusion to oppose the bolt
       Against my coming in: thou better know'st
       The offices of nature, bond of childhood,
       Effects of courtesy, dues of gratitude;
       Thy half o' the kingdom hast thou not forgot,
       Wherein I thee endow'd.

REG.   Good sir, to the purpose.
LEAR.   Who put my man i' the stocks?   [*Tucket within.*]
CORN.   What trumpet's that?
REG.   I know't; my sister's: this approves[20] her letter,
       That she would soon be here.

Enter OSWALD

                     Is your lady come?
LEAR.   This is a slave whose easy-borrow'd pride
       Dwells in the fickle grace of her he follows.
       Out, varlet, from my sight!
CORN.   What means your grace?
LEAR.   Who stock'd my servant? Regan, I have good hope
       Thou didst not know on't. Who comes here?

Enter GONERIL

                      O heavens,
       If you do love old men, if your sweet sway
       Allow[21] obedience, if yourselves are old,
       Make it your cause; send down, and take my part!
       [*To Gon.*] Art not ashamed to look upon this beard?
       O Regan, wilt thou take her by the hand?
GON.   Why not by the hand, sir? How have I offended?
       All's not offence that indiscretion finds[22]
       And dotage terms so.
LEAR.   O sides, you are too tough;
       Will you yet hold? How came my man i' the stocks?
CORN.   I set him there, sir: but his own disorders
       Deserved much less advancement.
LEAR.   You! did you?

---

20. *approves*] corroborates, confirms.
21. *Allow*] Approve of.
22. *finds*] judges, esteems.

REG.   I pray you, father, being weak, seem so.
If, till the expiration of your month,
You will return and sojourn with my sister,
Dismissing half your train, come then to me:
I am now from home and out of that provision
Which shall be needful for your entertainment.

LEAR.   Return to her, and fifty men dismiss'd?
No, rather I abjure all roofs, and choose
To wage against the enmity o' the air,
To be a comrade with the wolf and owl, —
Necessity's sharp pinch! Return with her?
Why, the hot-blooded France, that dowerless took
Our youngest born, I could as well be brought
To knee his throne, and, squire-like, pension beg
To keep base life afoot. Return with her?
Persuade me rather to be slave and sumpter[23]
To this detested groom.   *[Pointing at Oswald.]*

GON.   At your choice, sir.

LEAR.   I prithee, daughter, do not make me mad:
I will not trouble thee, my child; farewell:
We'll no more meet, no more see one another:
But yet thou art my flesh, my blood, my daughter;
Or rather a disease that 's in my flesh,
Which I must needs call mine: thou art a boil,
A plague-sore, an embossed[24] carbuncle,
In my corrupted blood. But I'll not chide thee;
Let shame come when it will, I do not call it:
I do not bid the thunder-bearer shoot,
Nor tell tales of thee to high-judging Jove:
Mend when thou canst; be better at thy leisure:
I can be patient; I can stay with Regan,
I and my hundred knights.

REG.   Not altogether so:
I look'd not for you yet, nor am provided
For your fit welcome. Give ear, sir, to my sister;

---

23. *sumpter*] literally a pack-horse, but often found in the sense of "drudge."
24. *embossed*] swollen.

For those that mingle reason with your passion
Must be content to think you old, and so —
But she knows what she does.

LEAR.   Is this well spoken?

REG.   I dare avouch it, sir: what, fifty followers?
Is it not well? What should you need of more?
Yea, or so many, sith that both charge[25] and danger
Speak 'gainst so great a number? How in one house
Should many people under two commands
Hold amity? 'T is hard, almost impossible.

GON.   Why might not you, my lord, receive attendance
From those that she calls servants or from mine?

REG.   Why not, my lord? If then they chanced to slack you,
We could control them. If you will come to me,
For now I spy a danger, I entreat you
To bring but five and twenty: to no more
Will I give place or notice.

LEAR.   I gave you all —

REG.   And in good time you gave it.

LEAR.   Made you my guardians, my depositaries,[26]
But kept a reservation[27] to be follow'd
With such a number. What, must I come to you
With five and twenty, Regan? said you so?

REG.   And speak 't again, my lord; no more with me.

LEAR.   Those wicked creatures yet do look well-favour'd,
When others are more wicked; not being the worst
Stands in some rank of praise. [*To Gon.*] I'll go with thee:
Thy fifty yet doth double five and twenty,
And thou art twice her love.

GON.   Hear me, my lord:
What need you five and twenty, ten, or five,
To follow in a house where twice so many
Have a command to tend you?

REG.   What need one?

---

25. *charge*] expense.
26. *depositaries*] trustees.
27. *reservation*] used in the legal sense of saving clause.

LEAR.   O, reason not the need: our basest beggars
         Are in the poorest thing superfluous:[28]
         Allow not nature more than nature needs,
         Man's life 's as cheap as beast's: thou art a lady;
         If only to go warm were gorgeous,
         Why, nature needs not what thou gorgeous wear'st,
         Which scarcely keeps thee warm. But for true need,—
         You heavens, give me that patience, patience I need!
         You see me here, you gods, a poor old man,
         As full of grief as age; wretched in both:
         If it be you that stirs these daughters' hearts
         Against their father, fool me not so much
         To bear it tamely; touch me with noble anger,
         And let not women's weapons, water-drops,
         Stain my man's cheeks! No, you unnatural hags,
         I will have such revenges on you both
         That all the world shall—I will do such things,—
         What they are, yet I know not, but they shall be
         The terrors of the earth. You think I'll weep;
         No, I'll not weep:
         I have full cause of weeping; but this heart
         Shall break into a hundred thousand flaws,
         Or ere I'll weep. O fool, I shall go mad!
                      [*Exeunt Lear, Gloucester, Kent, and Fool.*]
CORN.   Let us withdraw; 't will be a storm.
                                          [*Storm and tempest.*]

REG.   This house is little: the old man and his people
         Cannot be well bestow'd.
GON.   'T is his own blame; hath put himself from rest,
         And must needs taste his folly.
REG.   For his particular, I'll receive him gladly,
         But not one follower.
GON.   So am I purposed.
         Where is my lord of Gloucester?
CORN.   Follow'd the old man forth: he is return'd.

———————

28. *Are . . . superfluous*] Have in the very depths of poverty something above their actual
   need.

Re-enter GLOUCESTER

GLOU.   The king is in high rage.
CORN.   Whither is he going?
GLOU.   He calls to horse; but will I know not whither.
CORN.   'T is best to give him way; he leads himself.
GON.   My lord, entreat him by no means to stay.
GLOU.   Alack, the night comes on, and the bleak winds
        Do sorely ruffle; for many miles about
        There's scarce a bush.
REG.   O, sir, to wilful men
        The injuries that they themselves procure
        Must be their schoolmasters. Shut up your doors:
        He is attended with a desperate train;[29]
        And what they may incense him to, being apt
        To have his ear abused, wisdom bids fear.
CORN.   Shut up your doors, my lord; 't is a wild night:
        My Regan counsels well: come out o' the storm.

                                              [*Exeunt.*]

---

29. *He is attended ... train*] Regan appears to falsify the present facts. Lear departs
   unattended by any train of followers. The fool is now the king's only companion.

ACT III

SCENE I — A *Heath*

Storm still. Enter KENT *and a* Gentleman, *meeting*

KENT.   Who's there, besides foul weather?
GENT.   One minded like the weather, most unquietly.
KENT.   I know you. Where's the king?
GENT.   Contending with the fretful elements;
     Bids the wind blow the earth into the sea,
     Or swell the curled waters 'bove the main,[1]
     That things might change or cease; tears his white hair,
     Which the impetuous blasts, with eyeless rage,
     Catch in their fury, and make nothing of;
     Strives in his little world of man to out-scorn
     The to-and-fro-conflicting wind and rain.
     This night, wherein the cub-drawn[2] bear would couch,
     The lion and the belly-pinched wolf
     Keep their fur dry, unbonneted he runs,
     And bids what will take all.
KENT.   But who is with him?
GENT.   None but the fool; who labours to out-jest
     His heart-struck injuries.
KENT.   Sir, I do know you;
     And dare, upon the warrant of my note,[3]
     Commend a dear thing[4] to you. There is division,

---

1. *main*] mainland.
2. *cub-drawn*] sucked dry by the cubs, and thereby rendered hungry and ferocious.
3. *upon the warrant of my note*] on the strength of my knowledge of you.
4. *a dear thing*] an urgent, desperate matter.

55

Although as yet the face of it be cover'd
With mutual cunning, 'twixt Albany and Cornwall;
Who have — as who have not, that their great stars
Throned and set high? — servants, who seem no less,
Which are to France the spies and speculations
Intelligent of our state; what hath been seen,
Either in snuffs and packings[5] of the dukes,
Or the hard rein which both of them have borne
Against the old kind king, or something deeper,
Whereof perchance these are but furnishings,[6] —
But true it is, from France there comes a power[7]
Into this scatter'd kingdom; who already,
Wise in our negligence, have secret feet[8]
In some of our best ports, and are at point
To show their open banner. Now to you:
If on my credit you dare build so far
To make your speed to Dover, you shall find
Some that will thank you, making just report
Of how unnatural and bemadding sorrow
The king hath cause to plain.[9]
I am a gentleman of blood and breeding,
And from some knowledge and assurance offer
This office to you.

GENT.   I will talk further with you.

KENT.   No, do not.
For confirmation that I am much more
Than my out-wall,[10] open this purse and take
What it contains. If you shall see Cordelia, —
As fear not but you shall, — show her this ring,
And she will tell you who your fellow is
That yet you do not know. Fie on this storm!

---

5. *snuffs and packings*] jealous quarrels and underhand intrigues.
6. *furnishings*] trimmings, appendages.
7. *a power*] a military force.
8. *have secret feet*] have secretly set foot.
9. *plain*] complain.
10. *out-wall*] exterior.

I will go seek the king.
GENT.   Give me your hand:
Have you no more to say?
KENT.   Few words, but, to effect, more than all yet;
That when we have found the king, — in which your pain
That way, I'll this,[11] — he that first lights on him
Holla the other.   [*Exeunt severally.*]

SCENE II — *Another Part of the Heath*

Storm Still

Enter LEAR *and* Fool

LEAR.   Blow, winds, and crack your cheeks! rage! blow!
You cataracts and hurricanoes, spout
Till you have drench'd our steeples, drown'd the cocks![1]
You sulphurous and thought-executing[2] fires,
Vaunt-couriers[3] to oak-cleaving thunderbolts,
Singe my white head! And thou, all-shaking thunder,
Smite flat the thick rotundity o' the world!
Crack nature's moulds, all germins[4] spill at once
That make ingrateful man!
FOOL.   O nuncle, court holy-water[5] in a dry house is better than this
rain-water out o' door. Good nuncle, in, and ask thy daughters'
blessing: here's a night pities neither wise man nor fool.
LEAR.   Rumble thy bellyful! Spit, fire! spout, rain!
Nor rain, wind, thunder, fire, are my daughters:

---

11. *in which your pain . . . I'll this*] in which your endeavors shall take that way, while I'll
take this direction.

---

1. *cocks*] the cocks on the tops of steeples.
2. *thought-executing*] working with the rapidity of thought.
3. *Vaunt-couriers*] Heralds, forerunners.
4. *germins*] seeds.
5. *court holy-water*] flattering speeches.

I tax not you, you elements, with unkindness;
I never gave you kingdom, call'd you children,
You owe me no subscription:[6] then let fall
Your horrible pleasure; here I stand, your slave,
A poor, infirm, weak and despised old man:
But yet I call you servile ministers,
That have with two pernicious daughters join'd
Your high-engender'd battles[7] 'gainst a head
So old and white as this. O! O! 't is foul!

FOOL.   He that has a house to put's head in has a good head-piece.

> The cod-piece that will house
>   Before the head has any,
> The head and he shall louse
>   So beggars marry many.
> The man that makes his toe
>   What he his heart should make
> Shall of a corn cry woe,
>   And turn his sleep to wake.[8]

For there was never yet fair woman but she made mouths in a glass.

LEAR.   No, I will be the pattern of all patience;
I will say nothing.

Enter KENT

KENT.   Who's there?
FOOL.   Marry, here's grace and a cod-piece; that's a wise man and a fool.
KENT.   Alas, sir, are you here? things that love night
Love not such nights as these; the wrathful skies
Gallow[9] the very wanderers of the dark,
And make them keep their caves: since I was man,
Such sheets of fire, such bursts of horrid thunder,

---

6. *subscription*] allegiance.
7. *high-engender'd battles*] armies bred on high (i.e., in the sky); battalions recruited in the heavens.
8. *The man . . . wake*] The general meaning is that the man who cherishes a mean part of his being, instead of a really vital part, is likely to suffer pain from the very part to which he shows the unwise preference.
9. *Gallow*] Frighten.

Such groans of roaring wind and rain, I never
Remember to have heard: man's nature cannot carry
The affliction nor the fear.

LEAR.   Let the great gods,
That keep this dreadful pother o'er our heads,
Find out their enemies now. Tremble, thou wretch,
That hast within thee undivulged crimes,
Unwhipp'd of justice: hide thee, thou bloody hand;
Thou perjured, and thou simular[10] man of virtue
That art incestuous: caitiff, to pieces shake,
That under covert and convenient seeming[11]
Hast practised on man's life: close pent-up guilts,
Rive your concealing continents and cry
These dreadful summoners grace. I am a man
More sinn'd against than sinning.

KENT.   Alack, bare-headed!
Gracious my lord, hard by here is a hovel;
Some friendship will it lend you 'gainst the tempest:
Repose you there; while I to this hard house —
More harder than the stones whereof 't is raised;
Which even but now, demanding after you,
Denied me to come in — return, and force
Their scanted courtesy.

LEAR.   My wits begin to turn.
Come on, my boy: how dost, my boy? art cold?
I am cold myself. Where is this straw, my fellow?
The art[12] of our necessities is strange,
That can make vile things precious. Come, your hovel.
Poor fool and knave, I have one part in my heart
That's sorry yet for thee.

FOOL.   [*Singing*]

         He that has and a little tiny wit, —
         With hey, ho, the wind and the rain, —
         Must make content with his fortunes fit,
         For the rain it raineth every day.

---

10. *simular*] simulating.
11. *seeming*] hypocrisy.
12. *art*] alchemy.

LEAR.   True, my good boy. Come, bring us to this hovel.

[Exeunt Lear and Kent.]

FOOL.   This is a brave night to cool a courtezan. I'll speak a prophecy
ere I go:

> When priests are more in word than matter;
> When brewers mar their malt with water;
> When nobles are their tailors' tutors;
> No heretics burn'd, but wenches' suitors;
> When every case in law is right;
> No squire in debt, nor no poor knight;
> When slanders do not live in tongues,
> Nor cutpurses come not to throngs;
> When usurers tell their gold i' the field,
> And bawds and whores do churches build;
> Then shall the realm of Albion
> Come to great confusion:
> Then comes the time, who lives to see 't,
> That going shall be used with feet.

This prophecy Merlin shall make; for I live before his time. [*Exit.*]

SCENE III — *Gloucester's Castle*

Enter GLOUCESTER *and* EDMUND

GLOU.   Alack, alack, Edmund, I like not this unnatural dealing.
When I desired their leave that I might pity him, they took from me
the use of mine own house; charged me, on pain of their perpetual
displeasure, neither to speak of him, entreat for him, nor any way
sustain him.

EDM.   Most savage and unnatural!

GLOU.   Go to; say you nothing. There's a division betwixt the dukes,
and a worse matter than that: I have received a letter this night; 't is
dangerous to be spoken; I have locked the letter in my closet: these
injuries the king now bears will be revenged home; there is part of a
power already footed:[1] we must incline to the king. I will seek him

---

1. *a power already footed*] a military force has already landed.

and privily relieve him: go you, and maintain talk with the duke, that my charity be not of him perceived: if he ask for me, I am ill and gone to bed. Though I die for it, as no less is threatened me, the king my old master must be relieved. There is some strange thing toward, Edmund; pray you, be careful.

[*Exit.*]

EDM.   This courtesy, forbid thee, shall the duke
           Instantly know, and of that letter too:
           This seems a fair deserving,[2] and must draw me
           That which my father loses; no less than all:
           The younger rises when the old doth fall.   [*Exit.*]

SCENE IV — *The Heath*

Before a Hovel

Enter LEAR, KENT, *and* Fool

KENT.   Here is the place, my lord: good my lord, enter:
          The tyranny of the open night 's too rough
          For nature to endure.   [*Storm still.*]
LEAR.   Let me alone.
KENT.   Good my lord, enter here.
LEAR.   Wilt break my heart?
KENT.   I had rather break mine own. Good my lord, enter.
LEAR.   Thou think'st 't is much that this contentious storm
          Invades us to the skin: so 't is to thee;
          But where the greater malady is fix'd
          The lesser is scarce felt. Thou'ldst shun a bear,
          But if thy flight lay toward the raging sea
          Thou'ldst meet the bear i' the mouth. When the mind's free
          The body's delicate: the tempest in my mind
          Doth from my senses take all feeling else

---

2. *a fair deserving*] an action deserving fair recognition.

                Save what beats there. Filial ingratitude!
                Is it not as this mouth should tear this hand
                For lifting food to 't? But I will punish home.
                No, I will weep no more. In such a night
                To shut me out! Pour on; I will endure.
                In such a night as this! O Regan, Goneril!
                Your old kind father, whose frank heart gave you all, —
                O, that way madness lies; let me shun that;
                No more of that.
KENT.   Good my lord, enter here.
LEAR.   Prithee, go in thyself; seek thine own ease:
                This tempest will not give me leave to ponder
                On things would hurt me more. But I'll go in.
                [*To the Fool*] In, boy; go first. You houseless poverty,[1] —
                Nay, get thee in. I'll pray, and then I'll sleep.
                                         [*Fool goes in.*]

                Poor naked wretches, wheresoe'er you are,
                That bide the pelting of this pitiless storm,
                How shall your houseless heads and unfed sides,
                Your loop'd and window'd[2] raggedness, defend you
                From seasons such as these? O, I have ta'en
                Too little care of this! Take physic, pomp;
                Expose thyself to feel what wretches feel,
                That thou mayst shake the superflux to them
                And show the heavens more just.
EDG.   [*Within*] Fathom and half, fathom and half![3]
                Poor Tom!   [*The Fool runs out from the hovel.*]
FOOL.   Come not in here, nuncle, here's a spirit. Help me, help me!
KENT.   Give me thy hand. Who's there?
FOOL.   A spirit, a spirit: he says his name's poor Tom.
KENT.   What art thou that dost grumble there i' the straw?
                Come forth.

Enter EDGAR *disguised as a madman*

---

1. *poverty*] poor creature, pauper, beggar.
2. *loop'd and window'd*] full of holes and apertures.
3. *Fathom and half*] Perhaps Edgar refers to the depth of the flood of rain from which he is taking refuge in the hovel.

EDG.   Away! the foul fiend follows me!

        Through the sharp hawthorn blows the cold wind.

        Hum! go to thy cold bed and warm thee.

LEAR.   Hast thou given all to thy two daughters? and art thou come to this?

EDG.   Who gives any thing to poor Tom? whom the foul fiend hath led through fire and through flame, through ford and whirlpool, o'er bog and quagmire; that hath laid knives under his pillow and halters in his pew; set ratsbane by his porridge;[4] made him proud of heart, to ride on a bay trotting-horse over four-inched bridges, to course his own shadow for a traitor. Bless thy five wits! Tom's a-cold. O, do de, do de, do de. Bless thee from whirlwinds, star-blasting, and taking![5] Do poor Tom some charity, whom the foul fiend vexes. There could I have him now, and there, and there again, and there.   [*Storm still.*]

LEAR.   What, have his daughters brought him to this pass?

        Couldst thou save nothing? Didst thou give them all?

FOOL.   Nay, he reserved a blanket, else we had been all shamed.

LEAR.   Now, all the plagues that in the pendulous air

        Hang fated o'er men's faults light on thy daughters!

KENT.   He hath no daughters, sir.

LEAR.   Death, traitor! nothing could have subdued nature

        To such a lowness but his unkind daughters.

        Is it the fashion that discarded fathers

        Should have thus little mercy on their flesh?

        Judicious punishment! 't was this flesh begot

        Those pelican daughters.[6]

EDG.   Pillicock sat on Pillicock-hill:[7]

                   Halloo, halloo, loo, loo!

FOOL.   This cold night will turn us all to fools and madmen.

EDG.   Take heed o' the foul fiend: obey thy parents; keep thy word

---

4. *laid knives . . . by his porridge*] The devil was popularly credited with placing such temptations to suicide in the way of the possessed or the insane.

5. *taking*] bewitchment, infection by witches.

6. *pelican daughters*] The young of the pelican was commonly credited with drinking its parent's blood.

7. *Pillicock . . . Pillicock-hill*] A nursery rhyme. "Pillicock," which had a double meaning, was often used as a term of endearment for children.

justly; swear not; commit not with man's sworn spouse; set not thy
sweet heart on proud array. Tom's a-cold.

LEAR.　　What hast thou been?

EDG.　　A serving-man, proud in heart and mind; that curled my hair;
wore gloves in my cap; served the lust of my mistress' heart and did
the act of darkness with her; swore as many oaths as I spake words
and broke them in the sweet face of heaven: one that slept in the
contriving of lust and waked to do it: wine loved I deeply, dice
dearly, and in woman out-paramoured the Turk: false of heart, light
of ear,[8] bloody of hand; hog in sloth, fox in stealth, wolf in greedi-
ness, dog in madness, lion in prey. Let not the creaking of shoes nor
the rustling of silks betray thy poor heart to woman: keep thy foot
out of brothels, thy hand out of plackets,[9] thy pen from lenders'
books, and defy the foul fiend.

　　　　　"Still through the hawthorn blows the cold wind."
　　　　　Says suum, mun, ha, no, nonny.
　　　　　Dolphin my boy, my boy, sessa! let him trot by.

　　　　　　　　　　　　　　　　　　　　　　　[Storm still.]

LEAR.　　Why, thou wert better in thy grave than to answer with thy
uncovered body this extremity of the skies. Is man no more than
this? Consider him well. Thou owest the worm no silk, the beast no
hide, the sheep no wool, the cat no perfume. Ha! here's three on 's
are sophisticated.[10] Thou art the thing itself: unaccommodated
man is no more but such a poor, bare, forked[11] animal as thou art.
Off, off, you lendings![12] come, unbutton here.

　　　　　　　　　　　　　　　　　　　[Tearing off his clothes.]

FOOL.　　Prithee, nuncle, be contented; 't is a naughty night to swim in.
Now a little fire in a wild field were like an old lecher's heart, a
small spark, all the rest on's body cold. Look, here comes a walking
fire.

Enter GLOUCESTER, *with a torch*

EDG.　　This is the foul fiend Flibbertigibbet:[13] he begins at curfew

---

　　8.　*light of ear*] credulous of slanderous gossip or of obscenity.
　　9.　*plackets*] the openings in petticoats.
　10.　*sophisticated*] artificially made up (by wearing clothes).
　11.　*forked*] two-pronged, two-legged.
　12.　*lendings*] borrowed clothes.
　13.　*Flibbertigibbet*] a traditional name of an imp or demon.

and walks till the first cock; he gives the web and the pin,[14] squints
the eye and makes the hare-lip; mildews the white wheat[15] and
hurts the poor creature of earth.

> Saint Withold footed thrice the 'old;[16]
> He met the night-mare and her nine-fold;[17]
> > Bid her alight,
> > And her troth plight,
> And aroint thee,[18] witch, aroint thee!

KENT.   How fares your grace?
LEAR.   What's he?
KENT.   Who's there? What is't you seek?
GLOU.   What are you there? Your names?
EDG.   Poor Tom, that eats the swimming frog, the toad, the tadpole,
the wall-newt and the water;[19] that in the fury of his heart, when
the foul fiend rages, eats cow-dung for sallets;[20] swallows the old rat
and the ditch-dog; drinks the green mantle of the standing pool;
who is whipped from tithing to tithing,[21] and stock-punished, and
imprisoned; who hath had three suits to his back, six shirts to his
body, horse to ride and weapon to wear;

> But mice and rats and such small deer
> Have been Tom's food for seven long year.

Beware my follower. Peace, Smulkin;[22] peace, thou fiend!
GLOU.   What, hath your grace no better company?
EDG.   The prince of darkness is a gentleman: Modo he's call'd, and
Mahu.[23]
GLOU.   Our flesh and blood is grown so vile, my lord,
That it doth hate what gets it.

---

14. *the web and the pin*] cataract of the eye.
15. *the white wheat*] the ripening wheat.
16. *Saint Withold . . . 'old*] No such saint apparently is noticed elsewhere, but he has been
doubtfully identified with Saint Vitalis, who was invoked against nightmares. "The
'old" clearly stands for "the wold," low-lying country.
17. *nine-fold*] nine foals.
18. *aroint thee*] begone.
19. *the water*] the water-newt.
20. *sallets*] salads.
21. *tithing*] district or parish.
22. *Smulkin*] the name of one of the fiends.
23. *Modo . . . Mahu*] names for devils.

EDG.   Poor Tom's a-cold.
GLOU.   Go in with me: my duty cannot suffer
          To obey in all your daughters' hard commands:
          Though their injunction be to bar my doors
          And let this tyrannous night take hold upon you,
          Yet have I ventured to come seek you out
          And bring you where both fire and food is ready.
LEAR.   First let me talk with this philosopher.
          What is the cause of thunder?
KENT.   Good my lord, take his offer; go into the house.
LEAR.   I'll talk a word with this same learned Theban.[24]
          What is your study?
EDG.   How to prevent the fiend and to kill vermin.
LEAR.   Let me ask you one word in private.
KENT.   Importune him once more to go, my lord;
          His wits begin to unsettle.
GLOU.   Canst thou blame him?
                                        [*Storm still.*]
          His daughters seek his death: ah, that good Kent!
          He said it would be thus, poor banish'd man!
          Thou say'st the king grows mad; I'll tell thee, friend,
          I am almost mad myself: I had a son,
          Now outlaw'd from my blood;[25] he sought my life,
          But lately, very late: I loved him, friend,
          No father his son dearer: truth to tell thee,
          The grief hath crazed my wits. What a night's this!
          I do beeseech your grace, —
LEAR.   O, cry you mercy, sir.
          Noble philosopher, your company.
EDG.   Tom's a-cold.
GLOU.   In, fellow, there, into the hovel: keep thee warm.
LEAR.   Come, let's in all.
KENT.   This way, my lord.
LEAR.   With him;
          I will keep still with my philosopher.

---

24. *learned Theban*] an ironical incoherence. A Theban or Boeotian — Thebes was the chief city of Boeotia — commonly connotes stupidity.
25. *outlaw'd from my blood*] disowned and disinherited.

KENT.   Good my lord, soothe him; let him take the fellow.
GLOU.   Take him you on.
KENT.   Sirrah, come on; go along with us.
LEAR.   Come, good Athenian.
GLOU.   No words, no words: hush.
EDG.

> Child Rowland to the dark tower came:
> His word was still "Fie, foh, and fum,
> I smell the blood of a British man."   *[Exeunt.]*

SCENE V — *Gloucester's Castle*

Enter CORNWALL *and* EDMUND

CORN.   I will have my revenge ere I depart his house.
EDM.   How, my lord, I may be censured, that nature thus gives way to
    loyalty, something fears me to think of.
CORN.   I now perceive, it was not altogether your brother's evil disposi-
    tion made him seek his death, but a provoking merit, set a-work by
    a reproveable badness in himself.
EDM.   How malicious is my fortune, that I must repent to be just!
    This is the letter he spoke of, which approves him an intelligent
    party to the advantages of France. O heavens! that this treason were
    not, or not I the detector!
CORN.   Go with me to the duchess.
EDM.   If the matter of this paper be certain, you have mighty busi-
    ness in hand.
CORN.   True or false, it hath made thee earl of Gloucester. Seek out
    where thy father is, that he may be ready for our apprehension.
EDM.   *[Aside]* If I find him comforting[1] the king, it will stuff his
    suspicion more fully. — I will persever in my course of loyalty,
    though the conflict be sore between that and my blood.[2]
CORN.   I will lay trust upon thee, and thou shalt find a dearer father in
    my love.   *[Exeunt.]*

---

1. *comforting*] supporting (as a legal accessory); the word is used in its legal sense.
2. *my blood*] my natural feeling.

SCENE VI — A *Chamber in a Farmhouse Adjoining the Castle*

Enter GLOUCESTER, LEAR, KENT, Fool, *and* EDGAR

GLOU.   Here is better than the open air; take it thankfully. I will piece out the comfort with what addition I can: I will not be long from you.

KENT.   All the power of his wits have given way to his impatience: the gods reward your kindness!

                                                              [*Exit Gloucester.*]

EDG.   Frateretto[1] calls me, and tells me Nero is an angler in the lake of darkness. Pray, innocent, and beware the foul fiend.

FOOL.   Prithee, nuncle, tell me whether a madman be a gentleman or a yeoman.

LEAR.   A king, a king!

FOOL.   No, he's a yeoman that has a gentleman to his son, for he's a mad yeoman that sees his son a gentleman before him.

LEAR.   To have a thousand with red burning spits
             Come hissing in upon 'em, —

EDG.   The foul fiend bites my back.

FOOL.   He's mad that trusts in the tameness of a wolf, a horse's health, a boy's love, or a whore's oath.

LEAR.   It shall be done; I will arraign them straight.
             [*To Edgar*] Come, sit thou here, most learned justicer;[2]
             [*To the Fool*] Thou, sapient sir, sit here. Now, you she foxes![3]

EDG.   Look, where he stands and glares! Wantest thou eyes at trial, madam?

FOOL.
                        Come o'er the bourn,[4] Bessy, to me.
                           Her boat hath a leak,
                           And she must not speak
                        Why she dares not come over to thee.

———————————

1. *Frateretto*] the name of a fiend.
2. *justicer*] justiciar, judge of a high court.
3. *she foxes*] addressed to Goneril or her sister.
4. *bourn*] brook, stream.

EDG.   The foul fiend haunts poor Tom in the voice of a nightingale.
         Hopdance[5] cries in Tom's belly for two white herring. Croak not,
         black angel; I have no food for thee.
KENT.   How do you, sir? Stand you not so amazed:
         Will you lie down and rest upon the cushions?
LEAR.   I'll see their trial first. Bring in the evidence.
         [*To Edgar*] Thou robed man of justice, take thy place;
         [*To the Fool*] And thou, his yoke-fellow of equity,
         Bench by his side. [*To Kent*] You are o' the commission;[6]
         Sit you too.
EDG.   Let us deal justly.

         Sleepest or wakest thou, jolly shepherd?
              Thy sheep be in the corn;
         And for one blast of thy minikin[7] mouth,
              Thy sheep shall take no harm.

         Pur! the cat is gray.
LEAR.   Arraign her first; 't is Goneril. I here take my oath before this
         honourable assembly, she kicked the poor king her father.
FOOL.   Come hither, mistress. Is your name Goneril?
LEAR.   She cannot deny it.
FOOL.   Cry you mercy, I took you for a joint-stool.
LEAR.   And here's another, whose warp'd looks proclaim
         What store her heart is made on. Stop her there!
         Arms, arms, sword, fire! Corruption in the place!
         False justicer, why hast thou let her 'scape?
EDG.   Bless thy five wits!
KENT.   O pity! Sir, where is the patience now,
         That you so oft have boasted to retain?
EDG.   [*Aside*] My tears begin to take his part so much,
         They'll mar my counterfeiting.
LEAR.   The little dogs and all,
         Tray, Blanch, and Sweet-heart, see, they bark at me.
EDG.   Tom will throw his head at them. Avaunt, you curs!

---

5. *Hopdance*] the name of another fiend; possibly derived from the fiend Hobberdidaunce.
6. *the commission*] the commission of justices of the peace.
7. *minikin*] pretty, dainty.

> Be thy mouth or black or white,
> Tooth that poisons if it bite;
> Mastiff, greyhound, mongrel grim,
> Hound or spaniel, brach or lym,[8]
> Or bobtail tike or trundle-tail,[9]
> Tom will make them weep and wail:
> "For, with throwing thus my head,"
> Dogs leap the hatch,[10] and all are fled.

Do de, de, de. Sessa! Come, march to wakes and fairs and market-towns. Poor Tom, thy horn is dry.

LEAR.   Then let them anatomize Regan; see what breeds about her heart. Is there any cause in nature that makes these hard hearts? [*To Edgar*] You, sir, I entertain for one of my hundred; only I do not like the fashion of your garments. You will say they are Persian attire; but let them be changed.

KENT.   Now, good my lord, lie here and rest awhile.

LEAR.   Make no noise, make no noise; draw the curtains: so, so, so. We'll go to supper i' the morning. So, so, so.

FOOL.   And I'll go to bed at noon.

Re-enter GLOUCESTER

GLOU.   Come hither, friend: where is the king my master?

KENT.   Here, sir; but trouble him not: his wits are gone.

GLOU.   Good friend, I prithee, take him in thy arms;
         I have o'erheard a plot of death upon him:
         There is a litter ready; lay him in 't,
         And drive toward Dover, friend, where thou shalt meet
         Both welcome and protection. Take up thy master:
         If thou shouldst dally half an hour, his life,
         With thine and all that offer to defend him,
         Stand in assured loss. Take up, take up,
         And follow me, that will to some provision
         Give thee quick conduct.

KENT.   Oppressed nature sleeps.
         This rest might yet have balm'd thy broken sinews,[11]

---

8. *brach or lym*] bitch hound or bloodhound.
9. *trundle-tail*] a dog with a curled tail.
10. *the hatch*] the half-door.
11. *broken sinews*] shattered nerves.

Which, if convenience will not allow,
Stand in hard cure.[12] [*To the Fool*] Come, help to bear thy
    master;
Thou must not stay behind.

GLOU.   Come, come, away.
                         [*Exeunt all but Edgar.*]

EDG.   When we our betters see bearing our woes,
We scarcely think our miseries our foes.
Who alone suffers suffers most i' the mind,
Leaving free things[13] and happy shows behind:
But then the mind much sufferance doth o'erskip,
When grief hath mates, and bearing[14] fellowship.
How light and portable my pain seems now,
When that which makes me bend makes the king bow,
He childed as I father'd! Tom, away!
Mark the high noises, and thyself bewray[15]
When false opinion, whose wrong thought defiles thee,
In thy just proof repeals and reconciles thee.
What will hap more to-night, safe 'scape the king!
Lurk, lurk.   [*Exit.*]

---

12. *Stand in hard cure*] Must prove difficult to cure.
13. *free things*] things free of trouble.
14. *bearing*] suffering.
15. *bewray*] discover, reveal.

SCENE VII — *Gloucester's Castle*

Enter CORNWALL, REGAN, GONERIL, EDMUND, *and* Servants

CORN.   Post speedily to my lord your husband; show him this letter:[1]
         the army of France is landed. Seek out the traitor Gloucester.

                              [*Exeunt some of the Servants.*]

REG.   Hang him instantly.
GON.   Pluck out his eyes.
CORN.   Leave him to my displeasure. Edmund, keep you our sister
         company: the revenges we are bound to take upon your traitorous
         father are not fit for your beholding. Advise the duke, where you are
         going, to a most festinate[2] preparation: we are bound to the like.
         Our posts shall be swift and intelligent betwixt us. Farewell, dear
         sister: farewell, my lord of Gloucester.

Enter OSWALD

         How now! where's the king?
OSW.   My lord of Gloucester hath convey'd him hence:
         Some five or six and thirty of his knights,
         Hot questrists[3] after him, met him at gate;
         Who, with some other of the lords dependants,
         Are gone with him toward Dover; where they boast
         To have well-armed friends.
CORN.   Get horses for your mistress.
GON.   Farewell, sweet lord, and sister.
CORN.   Edmund, farewell.

                    [*Exeunt Goneril, Edmund, and Oswald.*]
                         Go seek the traitor Gloucester.
         Pinion him like a thief, bring him before us.

                              [*Exeunt other Servants.*]
         Though well we may not pass upon his life

---

1. *this letter*] the letter which Edmund has already given to Cornwall.
2. *festinate*] hurried.
3. *questrists*] searchers or pursuers (engaged in the quest); a very rare word.

        Without the form of justice, yet our power
        Shall do a courtesy to our wrath, which men
        May blame but not control. Who's there? the traitor?

Enter GLOUCESTER, *brought in by two or three*

REG.   Ingrateful fox! 't is he.
CORN.   Bind fast his corky⁴ arms.
GLOU.   What mean your graces? Good my friends, consider
        You are my guests: do me no foul play, friends.
CORN.   Bind him, I say.   *[Servants bind him.]*
REG.   Hard, hard. O filthy traitor!
GLOU.   Unmerciful lady as you are, I'm none.
CORN.   To this chair bind him. Villain, thou shalt find —
                            [Regan plucks his beard.]
GLOU.   By the kind gods, 't is most ignobly done
        To pluck me by the beard.
REG.   So white, and such a traitor!
GLOU.   Naughty lady,
        These hairs which thou dost ravish from my chin
        Will quicken⁵ and accuse thee: I am your host:
        With robbers' hands my hospitable favours⁶
        You should not ruffle thus. What will you do?
CORN.   Come, sir, what letters had you late from France?
REG.   Be simple answerer, for we know the truth.
CORN.   And what confederacy have you with the traitors
        Late footed in the kingdom?
REG.   To whose hands have you sent the lunatic king?
        Speak.
GLOU.   I have a letter guessingly set down,⁷
        Which came from one that's of a neutral heart,
        And not from one opposed.
CORN.   Cunning.
REG.   And false.
CORN.   Where hast thou sent the king?
GLOU.   To Dover.

---

4. *corky*] sapless, shrivelled with age.
5. *quicken*] assume life.
6. *my hospitable favours*] the face or features of me your host.
7. *guessingly set down*] written from conjecture.

REG.   Wherefore to Dover? Wast thou not charged at peril —
CORN.   Wherefore to Dover? Let him first answer that.
GLOU.   I am tied to the stake, and I must stand the course.[8]
REG.   Wherefore to Dover, sir?
GLOU.   Because I would not see thy cruel nails
        Pluck out his poor old eyes, nor thy fierce sister
        In his anointed flesh stick boarish fangs.
        The sea, with such a storm as his bare head
        In hell-black night endured, would have buoy'd up,
        And quench'd the stelled[9] fires:
        Yet, poor old heart, he holp[10] the heavens to rain.
        If wolves had at thy gate howl'd that stern time,
        Thou shouldst have said, "Good porter, turn the key,"
        All cruels else subscribed:[11] but I shall see
        The winged vengeance overtake such children.
CORN.   See 't shalt thou never. Fellows, hold the chair.
        Upon these eyes of thine I'll set my foot.
GLOU.   He that will think to live till he be old,
        Give me some help! O cruel! O you gods!
REG.   One side will mock another; the other too.
CORN.   If you see vengeance —
FIRST SERV.   Hold your hand, my lord:
        I have served you ever since I was a child;
        But better service have I never done you
        Than now to bid you hold.
REG.   How now, you dog!
FIRST SERV.   If you did wear a beard upon your chin,
        I'ld shake it on this quarrel. What do you mean?
CORN.   My villain![12]   [*They draw and fight.*]
FIRST SERV.   Nay, then, come on, and take the chance of anger.
REG.   Give me thy sword. A peasant stand up thus!
                    [*Takes a sword and runs at him behind.*]

---

   8. *the course*] the attack; the bout; the onset of dogs baiting the bear, according to the
      custom of the sport.
   9. *stelled*] probably "fixed," "everlasting."
  10. *holp*] helped.
  11. *All cruels else subscribed*] All their cruelty and fierceness in other circumstances being
      forgiven or condoned.
  12. *My villain*] My serf; one legally bound to me in ties of servitude.

FIRST SERV.   O, I am slain! My lord, you have one eye left
              To see some mischief on him. O!   [*Dies.*]
CORN.   Lest it see more, prevent it. Out, vile jelly!
          Where is thy lustre now?
GLOU.   All dark and comfortless. Where's my son Edmund?
          Edmund, enkindle all the sparks of nature,
          To quit[13] this horrid act.
REG.   Out, treacherous villain!
          Thou call'st on him that hates thee: it was he
          That made the overture[14] of thy treasons to us;
          Who is too good to pity thee.
GLOU.   O my follies! Then Edgar was abused.
          Kind gods, forgive me that, and prosper him!
REG.   Go thrust him out at gates, and let him smell
          His way to Dover. [*Exit one with Gloucester.*] How is't, my
              lord? how look you?
CORN.   I have received a hurt: follow me, lady.
          Turn out that eyeless villain: throw this slave
          Upon the dunghill. Regan, I bleed apace:
          Untimely comes this hurt: give me your arm.
                              [*Exit Cornwall, led by Regan.*]
SEC. SERV.   I'll never care what wickedness I do,
          If this man come to good.
THIRD SERV.   If she live long,
          And in the end meet the old course of death,
          Women will all turn monsters.
SEC. SERV.   Let 's follow the old earl, and get the Bedlam[15]
          To lead him where he would: his roguish madness
          Allows itself[16] to any thing.
THIRD SERV.   Go thou: I'll fetch some flax and whites of eggs
          To apply to his bleeding face. Now, heaven help him!
                              [*Exeunt severally.*]

----

13. *quit*] requite, repay.
14. *overture*] disclosure.
15. *the Bedlam*] the crazy beggar, Edgar.
16. *Allows itself*] Adapts itself, is amenable.

ACT IV

SCENE I — *The Heath*

Enter EDGAR

EDG.   Yet better thus, and known to be contemn'd,
           Than still contemn'd and flatter'd.[1] To be worst,
           The lowest and most dejected thing of fortune,
           Stands still in esperance,[2] lives not in fear:
           The lamentable change is from the best;
           The worst returns to laughter. Welcome then,
           Thou unsubstantial air that I embrace!
           The wretch that thou hast blown unto the worst
           Owes nothing to thy blasts. But who comes here?

Enter GLOUCESTER, *led by an* Old Man

           My father, poorly led? World, world, O world!
           But that thy strange mutations make us hate thee,
           Life would not yield to age.[3]

OLD MAN.   O, my good lord, I have been your tenant, and your father's
tenant, these fourscore years.

GLOU.   Away, get thee away; good friend, be gone:
           Thy comforts can do me no good at all;
           Thee they may hurt.

---

1. *Yet better . . . flatter'd*] The general meaning is, "It is better to know that one is despised than for one to be really despised and at the same time to be treated with false flattery which conceals the truth."
2. *esperance*] hope.
3. *But that . . . age*] If reverses of fortune did not make us despise existence altogether, we should never resign ourselves to the hateful incidents of infirm age. In other words, the world with all its uncertainties of fortune is such a repellent object to us that it doesn't really matter whether we are young or old, strong or weak.

OLD MAN.   Alack, sir, you cannot see your way.

GLOU.   I have no way and therefore want no eyes;
I stumbled when I saw: full oft 't is seen,
Our means secure[4] us, and our mere defects
Prove our commodities. Ah, dear son Edgar,
The food of thy abused father's wrath!
Might I but live to see thee in my touch,
I'ld say I had eyes again!

OLD MAN.   How now! Who's there?

EDG.   [*Aside*] O gods! Who is 't can say "I am at the worst"?
I am worse than e'er I was.

OLD MAN.   'T is poor mad Tom.

EDG.   [*Aside*] And worse I may be yet: the worst is not
So long as we can say "This is the worst."

OLD MAN.   Fellow, where goest?

GLOU.   Is it a beggar-man?

OLD MAN.   Madman and beggar too.

GLOU.   He has some reason, else he could not beg.
I' the last night's storm I such a fellow saw,
Which made me think a man a worm: my son
Came then into my mind, and yet my mind
Was then scarce friends with him: I have heard more since.
As flies to wanton boys, are we to the gods;
They kill us for their sport.

EDG.   [*Aside*] How should this be?
Bad is the trade that must play fool to sorrow,[5]
Angering itself and others. Bless thee, master!

GLOU.   Is that the naked fellow?

OLD MAN.   Ay, my lord.

GLOU.   Then, prithee, get thee gone: if for my sake
Thou wilt o'ertake us hence a mile or twain
I' the way toward Dover, do it for ancient love;
And bring some covering for this naked soul,
Who I'll entreat to lead me.

OLD MAN.   Alack, sir, he is mad.

---

4. *secure*] to render careless.
5. *play fool to sorrow*] divert sorrow by making merriment.

GLOU.   'T is the times' plague, when madmen lead the blind.
             Do as I bid thee, or rather do thy pleasure;
             Above the rest, be gone.
OLD MAN.   I'll bring him the best 'parel that I have,
             Come on 't what will.   [*Exit.*]
GLOU.   Sirrah, naked fellow, —
EDG.   Poor Tom's a-cold. [*Aside*] I cannot daub[6] it further.
GLOU.   Come hither, fellow.
EDG.   [*Aside*] And yet I must. — Bless thy sweet eyes, they bleed.
GLOU.   Know'st thou the way to Dover?
EDG.   Both stile and gate, horse-way and foot-path. Poor Tom hath
been scared out of his good wits. Bless thee, good man's son, from
the foul fiend! Five fiends have been in poor Tom at once; of lust,
as Obidicut; Hobbididence, prince of dumbness; Mahu, of steal-
ing; Modo, of murder; Flibbertigibbet,[7] of mopping and mowing;[8]
who since possesses chambermaids and waiting-women. So, bless
thee, master!
GLOU.   Here, take this purse, thou whom the heavens' plagues
             Have humbled to all strokes: that I am wretched
             Makes thee the happier. Heavens, deal so still!
             Let the superfluous and lust-dieted man,
             That slaves your ordinance, that will not see
             Because he doth not feel, feel your power quickly;
             So distribution should undo excess
             And each man have enough. Dost thou know Dover?
EDG.   Ay, master.
GLOU.   There is a cliff whose high and bending head
             Looks fearfully in the confined deep:
             Bring me but to the very brim of it,
             And I'll repair the misery thou dost bear
             With something rich about me: from that place
             I shall no leading need.
EDG.   Give me thy arm:
             Poor Tom shall lead thee.   [*Exeunt.*]

---

6. *daub*] disguise.
7. *Obidicut . . . Flibbertigibbet*] the names of five fiends.
8. *mopping and mowing*] grinning and grimacing (like an ape).

SCENE II — *Before the Duke of Albany's Palace*

Enter GONERIL *and* EDMUND

GON.   Welcome, my lord: I marvel our mild husband
            Not met us on the way.

Enter Oswald

                               Now, where's your master?
OSW.   Madam, within; but never man so changed.
            I told him of the army that was landed;
            He smiled at it: I told him you were coming;
            His answer was, "The worse:" of Gloucester's treachery
            And of the loyal service of his son
            When I inform'd him, then he call'd me sot[1]
            And told me I had turn'd the wrong side out:[2]
            What most he should dislike seems pleasant to him;
            What like, offensive.
GON.   [*To Edm.*] Then shall you go no further.
            It is the cowish terror of his spirit,
            That dares not undertake: he'll not feel wrongs,
            Which tie him to an answer. Our wishes on the way
            May prove effects. Back, Edmund, to my brother;
            Hasten his musters and conduct his powers:
            I must change arms[3] at home and give the distaff
            Into my husband's hands. This trusty servant
            Shall pass between us: ere long you are like to hear,
            If you dare venture in your own behalf,
            A mistress's command. Wear this; spare speech;
                                    [*Giving a favour.*]
            Decline your head: this kiss, if it durst speak,
            Would stretch thy spirits up into the air:
            Conceive, and fare thee well.

---

1. *sot*] fool.
2. *turn'd the wrong side out*] completely misinterpreted the facts.
3. *change arms*] exchange implements (*i.e.*, spears for spindles).

EDM.   Yours in the ranks of death.
GON.   My most dear Gloucester!

                                     [*Exit Edmund.*]

         O, the difference of man and man!
         To thee a woman's services are due:
         My fool usurps my body.
OSW.   Madam, here comes my lord.

                                       [*Exit.*]

Enter Albany

GON.   I have been worth the whistle.[4]
ALB.   O Goneril!
         You are not worth the dust which the rude wind
         Blows in your face. I fear your disposition:
         That nature which contemns it origin
         Cannot be border'd certain in itself;
         She that herself will sliver and disbranch
         From her material sap,[5] perforce must wither
         And come to deadly use.
GON.   No more; the text is foolish.
ALB.   Wisdom and goodness to the vile seem vile:
         Filths savour but themselves. What have you done?
         Tigers, not daughters, what have you perform'd?
         A father, and a gracious aged man,
         Whose reverence even the head-lugg'd bear[6] would lick,
         Most barbarous, most degenerate! have you madded.
         Could my good brother suffer you to do it?
         A man, a prince, by him so benefited!
         If that the heavens do not their visible spirits
         Send quickly down to tame these vile offences,
         It will come,
         Humanity must perforce prey on itself,
         Like monsters of the deep.
GON.   Milk-liver'd man!

---

4. *I have been worth the whistle*] an adaptation of the common proverb, "A poor dog is not worth the whistling." Goneril usually received an elaborate welcome on her return home.
5. *material sap*] sap giving essential nourishment.
6. *the head-lugg'd bear*] the bear dragged about by a cord round its head, and thereby infuriated.

That bear'st a cheek for blows, a head for wrongs;
Who hast not in thy brows an eye discerning
Thine honour from thy suffering; that not know'st
Fools do those villains pity who are punish'd
Ere they have done their mischief.[7] Where's thy drum?
France spreads his banners in our noiseless land,
With plumed helm thy state begins to threat,
Whiles thou, a moral[8] fool, sit'st still and criest
"Alack, why does he so?"

ALB.   See thyself, devil!
Proper deformity seems not in the fiend
So horrid as in woman.

GON.   O vain fool!

ALB.   Thou changed and self-cover'd thing, for shame,
Be-monster not thy feature. Were 't my fitness
To let these hands obey my blood,[9]
They are apt enough to dislocate and tear
Thy flesh and bones: howe'er thou art a fiend,
A woman's shape doth shield thee.

GON.   Marry, your manhood! mew![10]

Enter a Messenger

ALB.   What news?

MESS.   O, my good lord, the Duke of Cornwall's dead,
Slain by his servant, going to put out
The other eye of Gloucester.

ALB.   Gloucester's eyes!

MESS.   A servant that he bred, thrill'd with remorse,[11]
Opposed against the act, bending his sword
To his great master; who thereat enraged
Flew on him and amongst them fell'd him dead,
But not without that harmful stroke which since

---

7. *Who hast not . . . mischief*] Whose eyes are not able to distinguish the injury to honour
in tamely suffering wrong; who does not know that only fools show pity for those
wretches who are punished before they have wrought the mischief they have designed.

8. *moral*] moralising.

9. *blood*] disposition or impulse.

10. *mew!*] a derisive interjection.

11. *remorse*] compassion.

                    Hath pluck'd him after.
ALB.   This shows you are above,
                    You justicers, that these our nether crimes
                    So speedily can venge. But, O poor Gloucester!
                    Lost he his other eye?
MESS.   Both, both, my lord.
                    This letter, madam, craves a speedy answer;
                    'T is from your sister.
GON.   [Aside] One way I like this well;
                    But being widow, and my Gloucester with her,
                    May all the building in my fancy pluck
                    Upon my hateful life:[12] another way,
                    The news is not so tart. — I'll read, and answer. [Exit.]
ALB.   Where was his son when they did take his eyes?
MESS.   Come with my lady hither.
ALB.   He is not here.
MESS.   No, my good lord; I met him back again.[13]
ALB.   Knows he the wickedness?
MESS.   Ay, my good lord; 't was he inform'd against him,
                    And quit the house on purpose, that their punishment
                    Might have the freer course.
ALB.   Gloucester, I live
                    To thank thee for the love thou show'dst the king,
                    And to revenge thine eyes. Come hither, friend:
                    Tell me what more thou know'st.   [Exeunt.]

---

12. *One way . . . hateful life*] Goneril's cruelty approves the death of Cornwall and the
    blinding of Gloucester. But seeing that her sister is now a widow and Edmund, whom
    she calls by his father's title, "my Gloucester," is in her sister's company, she fears that
    the design of killing her own husband and marrying Edmund herself may be foiled, and
    that the castle of her imagination may fall and crush her own life, which in its present
    condition is loathsome to her.
13. *back again*] on his way back.

SCENE III — *The French Camp Near Dover*

Enter Kent *and a* Gentleman

KENT.   Why the King of France is so suddenly gone back know you
the reason?

GENT.   Something he left imperfect in the state which since his
coming forth is thought of, which imports to the kingdom so much
fear and danger that his personal return was most required and
necessary.

KENT.   Who hath he left behind him general?

GENT.   The Marshal of France, Monsieur La Far.

KENT.   Did your letters pierce the queen to any demonstration of
grief?

GENT.   Ay, sir; she took them, read them in my presence,
And now and then an ample tear trill'd[1] down
Her delicate cheek: it seem'd she was a queen
Over her passion, who most rebel-like
Sought to be king o'er her.

KENT.   O, then it moved her.

GENT.   Not to a rage: patience and sorrow strove
Who should express her goodliest. You have seen
Sunshine and rain at once: her smiles and tears
Were like a better way: those happy smilets
That play'd on her ripe lip seem'd not to know
What guests were in her eyes; which parted thence
As pearls from diamonds dropp'd. In brief,
Sorrow would be a rarity most beloved,
If all could so become it.

KENT.   Made she no verbal question?

GENT.   Faith, once or twice she heaved the name of "father"
Pantingly forth, as if it press'd her heart;
Cried "Sisters! sisters! Shame of ladies! sisters!
Kent! father! sisters! What, i' the storm? i' the night?

---

1. *trill'd*] trickled.

Let pity not be believed!" There she shook
The holy water from her heavenly eyes,
And clamour moisten'd: then away she started
To deal with grief alone.

KENT.   It is the stars,
The stars above us, govern our conditions;
Else one self mate and mate^2 could not beget
Such different issues. You spoke not with her since?

GENT.   No.

KENT.   Was this before the king return'd?

GENT.   No, since.

KENT.   Well, sir, the poor distressed Lear 's i' the town;
Who sometime in his better tune remembers
What we are come about, and by no means
Will yield to see his daughter.

GENT.   Why, good sir?

KENT.   A sovereign shame so elbows him: his own unkindness
That stripp'd her from his benediction, turn'd her
To foreign casualties, gave her dear rights
To his dog-hearted daughters: these things sting
His mind so venomously that burning shame
Detains him from Cordelia.

GENT.   Alack, poor gentleman!

KENT.   Of Albany's and Cornwall's powers you heard not?

GENT.   'T is so; they are afoot.

KENT.   Well, sir, I'll bring you to our master Lear,
And leave you to attend him: some dear cause^3
Will in concealment wrap me up awhile;
When I am known aright, you shall not grieve
Lending me this acquaintance. I pray you, go
Along with me.   [*Exeunt.*]

---

2. *self mate and mate*] the same husband and wife.
3. *some dear cause*] some very good reason.

SCENE IV — *The Same*

A Tent

Enter, with drum and colours, CORDELIA, Doctor, *and* Soldiers

COR. Alack, 't is he: why, he was met even now
As mad as the vex'd sea; singing aloud;
Crown'd with rank fumiter and furrow-weeds,
With bur-docks, hemlock, nettles, cuckoo-flowers,
Darnel,[1] and all the idle weeds that grow
In our sustaining corn. A century send forth;
Search every acre in the high-grown field,
And bring him to our eye. [*Exit an Officer.*] What can man's
    wisdom
In the restoring his bereaved sense?
He that helps him take all my outward worth.
DOCT. There is means, madam:
Our foster-nurse of nature is repose,
The which he lacks: that to provoke in him,
Are many simples[2] operative, whose power
Will close the eye of anguish.
COR.   All blest secrets,
All you unpublish'd virtues of the earth,
Spring with my tears! be aidant and remediate[3]
In the good man's distress! Seek, seek for him;
Lest his ungovern'd rage dissolve the life
That wants the means to lead it.[4]

Enter a Messenger

---

1. *rank fumiter . . . bur-docks . . . cuckoo-flowers, Darnel*] Cf. *Hen.* V, V, ii, 44–46: "her fallow leas The *darnel*, hemlock and *rank fumitory* Doth root upon." "Fumiter" is a common sort of weed, of which there seem to be five species known in England. *Burdocks*, or "burdock," is a coarse flower bearing prickly flowerheads called "burs," and having large dock-leaves. "Cuckoo flowers" is applied to many plants flowering in the spring. "Darnel" is raygrass, a weed often found in open cornfields.
2. *simples*] medicinal herbs.
3. *aidant and remediate*] helpful and remedial.
4. *the means to lead it*] the control of reason to guide it.

MESS.   News, madam;
      The British powers are marching hitherward.
COR.   'T is known before; our preparation stands
      In expectation of them. O dear father,
      It is thy business that I go about;
      Therefore great France
      My mourning and important tears[5] hath pitied.
      No blown ambition doth our arms incite,
      But love, dear love, and our aged father's right:
      Soon may I hear and see him!
      [*Exeunt.*]

SCENE V — *Gloucester's Castle*

Enter REGAN *and* OSWALD

REG.   But are my brother's powers set forth?
OSW.   Ay, madam.
REG.   Himself in person there?
OSW.   Madam, with much ado:
      Your sister is the better soldier.
REG.   Lord Edmund spake not with your lord at home?
OSW.   No, madam.
REG.   What might import my sister's letter to him?
OSW.   I know not, lady.
REG.   Faith, he is posted hence on serious matter.
      It was great ignorance, Gloucester's eyes being out,
      To let him live: where he arrives he moves
      All hearts against us: Edmund, I think, is gone,
      In pity of his misery, to dispatch
      His nighted life; moreover, to descry
      The strength o' the enemy.

---

5. *important tears*] importunate tears.

OSW.   I must needs after him, madam, with my letter.
REG.   Our troops set forth to-morrow: stay with us;
       The ways are dangerous.
OSW.   I may not, madam:
       My lady charged my duty in this business.
REG.   Why should she write to Edmund? Might not you
       Transport her purposes by word? Belike,
       Something — I know not what: I'll love thee much,
       Let me unseal the letter.
OSW.   Madam, I had rather —
REG.   I know your lady does not love her husband;
       I am sure of that: and at her late being here
       She gave strange œillades[1] and most speaking looks
       To noble Edmund. I know you are of her bosom.[2]
OSW.   I, madam?
REG.   I speak in understanding: you are; I know't:
       Therefore I do advise you, take this note:
       My lord is dead; Edmund and I have talk'd;
       And more convenient is he for my hand
       Than for your lady's: you may gather more.
       If you do find him, pray you, give him this;
       And when your mistress hears thus much from you,
       I pray, desire her call her wisdom to her.
       So, fare you well.
       If you do chance to hear of that blind traitor,
       Preferment falls on him that cuts him off.
OSW.   Would I could meet him, madam! I should show
       What party I do follow.
REG.   Fare thee well.   [*Exeunt.*]

---

1. *œillades*] amorous glances.
2. *of her bosom*] in her confidence.

SCENE VI — *Fields Near Dover*

Enter GLOUCESTER, *and* EDGAR *dressed like a peasant*

GLOU.	When shall we come to the top of that same hill?
EDG.	You do climb up it now: look, how we labour.
GLOU.	Methinks the ground is even.
EDG.	Horrible steep.

EDG.   Horrible steep.
Hark, do you hear the sea?

GLOU.   No, truly.

EDG.   Why then your other senses grow imperfect
By your eyes' anguish.

GLOU.   So may it be indeed:
Methinks thy voice is alter'd, and thou speak'st
In better phrase and matter than thou didst.

EDG.   You're much deceived: in nothing am I changed
But in my garments.

GLOU.   Methinks you're better spoken.

EDG.   Come on, sir; here's the place: stand still. How fearful
And dizzy 't is to cast one's eyes so low!
The crows and choughs[1] that wing the midway air
Show scarce so gross as beetles: half way down
Hangs one that gathers samphire,[2] dreadful trade!
Methinks he seems no bigger than his head:
The fishermen that walk upon the beach
Appear like mice; and yond tall anchoring bark
Diminish'd to her cock;[3] her cock, a buoy
Almost too small for sight: the murmuring surge
That on the unnumber'd idle pebbles chafes
Cannot be heard so high. I'll look no more,

---

1. *choughs*] jackdaws.
2. *samphire*] a rock herb named after St. Pierre or St. Peter, which is much used for pickling. It is sometimes called "sea-fennel."
3. *cock*] a ship's small boat, often called cock-boat.

	Lest my brain turn and the deficient sight
	Topple down headlong.
GLOU.	Set me where you stand.
EDG.	Give me your hand: you are now within a foot
	Of the extreme verge: for all beneath the moon
	Would I not leap upright.
GLOU.	Let go my hand.
	Here, friend, 's another purse; in it a jewel
	Well worth a poor man's taking: fairies and gods
	Prosper it with thee! Go thou further off;
	Bid me farewell, and let me hear thee going.
EDG.	Now fare you well, good sir.
GLOU.	With all my heart.
EDG.	Why I do trifle thus with his despair
	Is done to cure it.
GLOU.	[*Kneeling*] O you mighty gods!
	This world I do renounce, and in your sights
	Shake patiently my great affliction off:
	If I could bear it longer and not fall
	To quarrel with your great opposeless wills,
	My snuff[4] and loathed part of nature should
	Burn itself out. If Edgar live, O bless him!
	Now, fellow, fare thee well. [*He falls forward.*]
EDG.	Gone, sir: farewell.
	And yet I know not how conceit[5] may rob
	The treasury of life, when life itself
	Yields to the theft: had he been where he thought,
	By this had thought been past. Alive or dead?
	Ho, you sir! friend! Hear you, sir! speak!
	Thus might he pass[6] indeed: yet he revives.
	What are you, sir?
GLOU.	Away, and let me die.
EDG.	Hadst thou been aught but gossamer, feathers, air,
	So many fathom down precipitating,
	Thou'dst shiver'd like an egg: but thou dost breathe;

---

4. *snuff*] refuse or dregs.
5. *conceit*] imagination, false impression.
6. *pass*] pass away, die.

Hast heavy substance; bleed'st not; speak'st; art sound.
Ten masts at each[7] make not the altitude
Which thou hast perpendicularly fell:
Thy life's a miracle. Speak yet again.

GLOU.   But have I fall'n, or no?

EDG.   From the dread summit of this chalky bourn.
Look up a-height; the shrill-gorged lark so far
Cannot be seen or heard: do but look up.

GLOU.   Alack, I have no eyes.
Is wretchedness deprived that benefit,
To end itself by death? 'T was yet some comfort,
When misery could beguile the tyrant's rage
And frustrate his proud will.

EDG.   Give me your arm:
Up: so. How is't? Feel you your legs? You stand.

GLOU.   Too well, too well.

EDG.   This is above all strangeness.
Upon the crown o' the cliff, what thing was that
Which parted from you?

GLOU.   A poor unfortunate beggar.

EDG.   As I stood here below, methought his eyes
Were two full moons; he had a thousand noses,
Horns whelk'd and waved like the enridged sea:[8]
It was some fiend; therefore, thou happy father,
Think that the clearest[9] gods, who make them honours
Of men's impossibilities, have preserved thee.

GLOU.   I do remember now: henceforth I'll bear
Affliction till it do cry out itself
"Enough, enough," and die. That thing you speak of,
I took it for a man; often 't would say
"The fiend, the fiend:" he led me to that place.

EDG.   Bear free and patient thoughts. But who comes here?

Enter LEAR, *fantastically dressed with wild flowers*

---

7. *Ten masts at each*] Ten masts fastened end to end.
8. *whelk'd and waved . . . sea*] twisted or convolved (like the shell of the whelk fish) and
fluted like the furrowed sea.
9. *clearest*] most pure or righteous.

            The safer sense will ne'er accommodate
            His master thus.[10]

LEAR. No, they cannot touch me for coining; I am the king himself.

EDG. O thou side-piercing[11] sight!

LEAR. Nature 's above art in that respect. There's your press-money.[12] That fellow handles his bow like a crow-keeper;[13] draw me a clothier's yard.[14] Look, look, a mouse! Peace, peace; this piece of toasted cheese will do 't. There's my gauntlet; I'll prove it on a giant. Bring up the brown bills.[15] O, well flown, bird![16] i' the clout, i' the clout:[17] hewgh! Give the word.[18]

EDG. Sweet marjoram.

LEAR. Pass.

GLOU. I know that voice.

LEAR. Ha! Goneril, with a white beard! They flattered me like a dog, and told me I had white hairs in my beard ere the black ones were there. To say "ay" and "no" to every thing that I said! "Ay" and "no" too was no good divinity. When the rain came to wet me once and the wind to make me chatter; when the thunder would not peace at my bidding; there I found 'em, there I smelt 'em out. Go to, they are not men o' their words: they told me I was every thing; 't is a lie, I am not ague-proof.

GLOU. The trick of that voice I do well remember:
            Is 't not the king?

LEAR.   Ay, every inch a king:
            When I do stare, see how the subject quakes.
            I pardon that man's life. What was thy cause?

---

10. *The safer sense . . . thus*] The saner sense or the reason would never allow one in full possession of it to dress himself up thus. "His master" would be in modern grammar "its master."

11. *side-piercing*] piercing the heart.

12. *There's your press-money*] Lear imagines himself a recruiting officer handing bounty money to men forcibly impressed.

13. *crow-keeper*] scarecrow.

14. *draw me a clothier's yard*] shoot an arrow the length of a clothier's yard measure.

15. *the brown bills*] the halberdiers, soldiers bearing halberds, which were painted brown to preserve them from rust.

16. *well flown, bird!*] the falconer's cry to the hawk.

17. *i' the clout*] the cry of the archer who hit the "clout," or the bull's eye or pin fixed in the centre of the butt or target.

18. *Give the word*] The mad king imagines himself a sentinel demanding the watchword of Edgar.

Adultery?
Thou shalt not die: die for adultery! No:
The wren goes to 't, and the small gilded fly
Does lecher in my sight.
Let copulation thrive; for Gloucester's bastard son
Was kinder to his father than my daughters
Got 'tween the lawful sheets.
To 't, luxury,[19] pell-mell! for I lack soldiers.
Behold yond simpering dame,
Whose face between her forks[20] presages snow,
That minces virtue and does shake the head
To hear of pleasure's name;
The fitchew,[21] nor the soiled horse,[22] goes to 't
With a more riotous appetite.
Down from the waist they are Centaurs,
Though women all above:
But to the girdle do the gods inherit,
Beneath is all the fiends';
There's hell, there's darkness, there's the sulphurous pit,
Burning, scalding, stench, consumption; fie, fie, fie! pah, pah!
Give me an ounce of civet,[23] good apothecary, to sweeten my
imagination: there's money for thee.

GLOU.   O, let me kiss that hand!
LEAR.   Let me wipe it first; it smells of mortality.
GLOU.   O ruin'd piece of nature! This great world
           Shall so wear out to nought. Dost thou know me?
LEAR.   I remember thine eyes well enough. Dost thou squiny[24] at
           me? No, do thy worst, blind Cupid; I'll not love. Read thou this
           challenge; mark but the penning on 't.
GLOU.   Were all the letters suns, I could not see one.
EDG.   I would not take this from report: it is,
           And my heart breaks at it.
LEAR.   Read.

---

19. *luxury*] lust.
20. *forks*] legs.
21. *fitchew*] polecat, often applied to a harlot.
22. *the soiled horse*] the horse turned out to new grass, which rendered him wanton.
23. *civet*] a musky perfume, obtained from the glands of the civet cat.
24. *squiny*] look asquint.

GLOU.   What, with the case of eyes?[25]

LEAR.   O, ho, are you there with me?[26] No eyes in your head, nor no
money in your purse? Your eyes are in a heavy case,[27] your purse in
a light: yet you see how this world goes.

GLOU.   I see it feelingly.

LEAR.   What, art mad? A man may see how this world goes with no
eyes. Look with thine ears: see how yond justice rails upon yond
simple thief. Hark, in thine ear: change places, and, handy-dandy,
which is the justice, which is the thief? Thou hast seen a farmer's
dog bark at a beggar?

GLOU.   Ay, sir.

LEAR.   And the creature run from the cur? There thou mightst behold the great image of authority: a dog's obeyed in office.
    Thou rascal beadle, hold thy bloody hand!
    Why dost thou lash that whore? Strip thine own back;
    Thou hotly lust'st to use her in that kind
    For which thou whip'st her. The usurer hangs the cozener.
    Through tatter'd clothes small vices do appear;
    Robes and furr'd gowns hide all. Plate sin with gold,
    And the strong lance of justice hurtless breaks;
    Arm it in rags, a pigmy's straw does pierce it.
    None does offend, none, I say, none; I'll able 'em:[28]
    Take that of me, my friend, who have the power
    To seal the accuser's lips. Get thee glass eyes,
    And, like a scurvy politician, seem
    To see the things thou dost not.
    Now, now, now, now: pull off my boots: harder, harder: so.

EDG.   O, matter and impertinency mix'd!
    Reason in madness!

LEAR.   If thou wilt weep my fortunes, take my eyes.
    I know thee well enough; thy name is Gloucester:
    Thou must be patient; we came crying hither:
    Thou know'st, the first time that we smell the air,

---

25. *with the case of eyes*] with the sockets which once held eyes.
26. *are you there with me?*] do you understand me?
27. *a heavy case*] a sad plight.
28. *I'll able 'em*] I'll answer or vouch for them.

	We wawl and cry. I will preach to thee: mark.
GLOU.	Alack, alack the day!
LEAR.	When we are born, we cry that we are come
	To this great stage of fools. This's a good block.[29]
	It were a delicate stratagem, to shoe
	A troop of horse with felt: I'll put 't in proof;
	And when I have stol'n upon these sons-in-law,
	Then, kill, kill, kill, kill, kill, kill!

Enter a Gentleman, *with* Attendants

GENT.	O, here he is: lay hand upon him. Sir,
	Your most dear daughter—
LEAR.	No rescue? What, a prisoner? I am even
	The natural fool of fortune. Use me well;
	You shall have ransom. Let me have a surgeon;
	I am cut to the brains.
GENT.	You shall have any thing.
LEAR.	No seconds? all myself?
	Why, this would make a man a man of salt,[30]
	To use his eyes for garden water-pots,
	Ay, and laying autumn's dust.
GENT.	Good sir,—
LEAR.	I will die bravely, like a smug[31] bridegroom. What!
	I will be jovial: come, come; I am a king,
	My masters, know you that.
GENT.	You are a royal one, and we obey you.
LEAR.	Then there 's life in 't. Nay, an you get it, you shall get it by
	running. Sa, sa, sa, sa.
	[*Exit running; Attendants follow.*]
GENT.	A sight most pitiful in the meanest wretch,
	Past speaking of in a king! Thou hast one daughter,
	Who redeems nature from the general curse

---

29. *This's a good block*] "Block" is frequently used for the mould on which a hat is fashioned, and thus for the hat itself.
30. *salt*] salt tears.
31. *smug*] spruce, without any depreciatory sense.

	Which twain have brought her to.
EDG.	Hail, gentle sir.
GENT.	Sir, speed you: what's your will?
EDG.	Do you hear aught, sir, of a battle toward?
GENT.	Most sure and vulgar: every one hears that,
	Which can distinguish sound.
EDG.	But, by your favour,
	How near's the other army?
GENT.	Near and on speedy foot; the main descry
	Stands on the hourly thought.
EDG.	I thank you, sir: that's all.
GENT.	Though that the queen on special cause is here,
	Her army is moved on.
EDG.	I thank you, sir.
	[Exit Gent.]
GLOU.	You ever-gentle gods, take my breath from me;
	Let not my worser spirit tempt me again
	To die before you please!
EDG.	Well pray you, father.
GLOU.	Now, good sir, what are you?
EDG.	A most poor man, made tame to fortune's blows;
	Who, by the art of known and feeling sorrows,
	Am pregnant to good pity. Give me your hand,
	I'll lead you to some biding.[32]
GLOU.	Hearty thanks;
	The bounty and the benison of heaven
	To boot, and boot!

Enter OSWALD

OSW.	A proclaim'd prize! Most happy!
	That eyeless head of thine was first framed flesh
	To raise my fortunes. Thou old unhappy traitor,
	Briefly thyself remember: the sword is out
	That must destroy thee.
GLOU.	Now let thy friendly hand
	Put strength enough to 't. *[Edgar interposes.]*
OSW.	Wherefore, bold peasant,
	Darest thou support a publish'd traitor? Hence!

---

32. *biding*] lodging.

Lest that the infection of his fortune take
Like hold on thee. Let go his arm.

EDG.   Chill[33] not let go, zir, without vurther 'casion.

OSW.   Let go, slave, or thou diest!

EDG.   Good gentleman, go your gait, and let poor volk pass. An chud
ha' been zwaggered out of my life, 't would not ha' been zo long as
't is by a vortnight. Nay, come not near th' old man; keep out, che
vor ye,[34] or I'se try whether your costard or my ballow[35] be the
harder: chill be plain with you.

OSW.   Out, dunghill!   [*They fight.*]

EDG.   Chill pick your teeth, zir: come; no matter vor your foins.[36]
                                                        [*Oswald falls.*]

OSW.   Slave, thou hast slain me. Villain, take my purse:
If ever thou wilt thrive, bury my body;
And give the letters which thou find'st about me
To Edmund earl of Gloucester; seek him out
Upon the British party. O, untimely death!
Death!   [*Dies.*]

EDG.   I know thee well: a serviceable villain,
As duteous[37] to the vices of thy mistress
As badness would desire.

GLOU.   What, is he dead?

EDG.   Sit you down, father; rest you.
Let 's see these pockets: the letters that he speaks of
May be my friends. He 's dead; I am only sorry
He had no other deathsman.[38] Let us see:
Leave, gentle wax; and, manners, blame us not:
To know our enemies' minds, we 'ld rip their hearts;
Their papers, is more lawful.

[*Reads*] "Let our reciprocal vows be remembered. You have many
opportunities to cut him off: if your will want not, time and place will
be fruitfully offered. There is nothing done, if he return the con-
queror: then am I the prisoner, and his bed my gaol; from the

---

33. *Chill*] I will.
34. *che vor ye*] I warn you.
35. *your costard or my ballow*] your head or my cudgel.
36. *foins*] thrusts in fencing.
37. *duteous*] obsequious, obedient.
38. *deathsman*] executioner.

loathed warmth whereof deliver me, and supply the place for your
labour.
    "Your—wife, so I would say—affectionate servant,
"GONERIL."

O undistinguish'd space of woman's will!
A plot upon her virtuous husband's life;
And the exchange my brother! Here, in the sands,
Thee I'll rake up,[39] the post unsanctified
Of murderous lechers; and in the mature time
With this ungracious paper strike the sight
Of the death-practised[40] duke: for him 't is well
That of thy death and business I can tell.

GLOU.   The king is mad: how stiff is my vile sense,
That I stand up, and have ingenious feeling[41]
Of my huge sorrows! Better I were distract:
So should my thoughts be sever'd from my griefs,
And woes by wrong imaginations lose
The knowledge of themselves.   *[Drum afar off.]*

EDG.   Give me your hand:
Far off, methinks, I hear the beaten drum:
Come, father, I'll bestow you with a friend.   *[Exeunt.]*

---

39. *rake up*] cover.
40. *death-practised*] whose death is plotted.
41. *ingenious feeling*] lively consciousness.

Scene VII — A *Tent in the French Camp. Lear on a Bed Asleep, Soft Music Playing; Gentleman, and Others Attending*

Enter CORDELIA, KENT, *and* Doctor

COR. O thou good Kent, how shall I live and work,
   To match thy goodness? My life will be too short,
   And every measure fail me.

KENT. To be acknowledged, madam, is o'erpaid.
   All my reports go with the modest truth,
   Nor more nor clipp'd, but so.

COR.   Be better suited:[1]
   These weeds are memories of those worser hours:
   I prithee, put them off.

KENT.   Pardon me, dear madam;
   Yet to be known shortens my made intent:
   My boon I make it, that you know me not
   Till time and I think meet.

COR. Then be 't so, my good lord. [*To the Doctor*] How does the
    king?

DOCT. Madam, sleeps still.

COR. O you kind gods,
   Cure this great breach in his abused nature!
   The untuned and jarring senses, O, wind up
   Of this child-changed father!

DOCT.   So please your majesty
   That we may wake the king: he hath slept long.

COR. Be govern'd by your knowledge, and proceed
   I' the sway of your own will. Is he array'd?

GENT. Ay, madam; in the heaviness of his sleep
   We put fresh garments on him.

DOCT. Be by, good madam, when we do awake him;

---

1. *suited*] dressed.

I doubt not of his temperance.[2]

COR.   Very well.

DOCT. Please you, draw near. Louder the music there!

COR.   O my dear father! Restoration hang
        Thy medicine on my lips, and let this kiss
        Repair those violent harms that my two sisters
        Have in thy reverence made!

KENT.   Kind and dear princess!

COR.   Had you not been their father, these white flakes[3]
        Had challenged pity of them. Was this a face
        To be opposed against the warring winds?
        To stand against the deep dread-bolted thunder?
        In the most terrible and nimble stroke
        Of quick, cross lightning? to watch — poor perdu![4] —
        With this thin helm? Mine enemy's dog,
        Though he had bit me, should have stood that night
        Against my fire; and wast thou fain, poor father,
        To hovel thee with swine and rogues forlorn,
        In short[5] and musty straw? Alack, alack!
        'T is wonder that thy life and wits at once
        Had not concluded all. He wakes; speak to him.

DOCT. Madam, do you; 't is fittest.

COR.   How does my royal lord? How fares your majesty?

LEAR.   You do me wrong to take me out o' the grave:
        Thou art a soul in bliss; but I am bound
        Upon a wheel of fire, that mine own tears
        Do scald like molten lead.

COR.   Sir, do you know me?

LEAR.   You are a spirit, I know: when did you die?

COR.   Still, still, far wide![6]

DOCT. He's scarce awake: let him alone awhile.

LEAR.   Where have I been? Where am I? Fair daylight?
        I am mightily abused. I should e'en die with pity,

---

2. *temperance*] sanity, calmness.
3. *white flakes*] snow-white hair.
4. *perdu*] from "enfans perdus" or "perdus," soldiers intrusted with very perilous service.
5. *short*] scanty, insufficient.
6. *wide*] astray.

        To see another thus. I know not what to say.
        I will not swear these are my hands: let's see;
        I feel this pin prick. Would I were assured
        Of my condition!

COR.   O, look upon me, sir,
        And hold your hands in benediction o'er me.
        No, sir, you must not kneel.

LEAR.   Pray, do not mock me:
        I am a very foolish fond old man,
        Fourscore and upward, not an hour more nor less;
        And, to deal plainly,
        I fear I am not in my perfect mind.
        Methinks I should know you and know this man;
        Yet I am doubtful; for I am mainly ignorant
        What place this is, and all the skill I have
        Remembers not these garments, nor I know not
        Where I did lodge last night. Do not laugh at me;
        For, as I am a man, I think this lady
        To be my child Cordelia.

COR.   And so I am, I am.
LEAR.   Be your tears wet? yes, faith. I pray, weep not:
        If you have poison for me, I will drink it.
        I know you do not love me; for your sisters
        Have, as I do remember, done me wrong:
        You have some cause, they have not.

COR.   No cause, no cause.
LEAR.   Am I in France?
KENT.   ꞌ   In your own kingdom, sir.
LEAR.   Do not abuse me.
DOCT.   Be comforted, good madam: the great rage,
        You see, is kill'd in him: and yet it is danger
        To make him even o'er[7] the time he has lost.
        Desire him to go in; trouble him no more
        Till further settling.

COR.   Will 't please your highness walk?[8]

---

7. *even o'er*] account for, bridge over in his recollection.
8. *walk*] withdraw.

LEAR.   You must bear with me. Pray you now, forget and forgive: I am
   old and foolish.

                              [*Exeunt all but Kent and Gentleman.*]

GENT.   Holds it true, sir, that the Duke of Cornwall was so slain?

KENT.   Most certain, sir.

GENT.   Who is conductor of his people?

KENT.   As 't is said, the bastard son of Gloucester.

GENT.   They say Edgar, his banished son, is with the Earl of Kent in
   Germany.

KENT.   Report is changeable. 'T is time to look about; the powers of
   the kingdom approach apace.

GENT.   The arbitrement[9] is like to be bloody. Fare you well, sir.

                                                        [*Exit.*]

KENT.   My point and period will be thoroughly wrought,
   Or well or ill, as this day's battle 's fought.[10]   [*Exit.*]

---

9. *arbitrement*] decision.

10. *My point and period . . . fought*] The aim and end of my life will be fully attained for
   either good or ill in the course of this day's battle.

ACT V

SCENE I — *The British Camp Near Dover*

Enter, with drum and colours, EDMUND, REGAN, Gentlemen, *and* Soldiers

EDM.   Know of the Duke if his last purpose hold,
       Or whether since he is advised by aught
       To change the course: he's full of alteration
       And self-reproving: bring his constant pleasure.[1]
       [*To a Gentleman, who goes out.*]
REG.   Our sister's man is certainly miscarried.
EDM.   'T is to be doubted,[2] madam.
REG.   Now, sweet lord,
       You know the goodness I intend upon you:
       Tell me, but truly, but then speak the truth,
       Do you not love my sister?
EDM.   In honour'd love.
REG.   But have you never found my brother's way
       To the forfended[3] place?
EDM.   That thought abuses you.
REG.   I am doubtful that you have been conjunct
       And bosom'd with her, as far as we call hers.
EDM.   No, by mine honour, madam.
REG.   I never shall endure her: dear my lord,

---

1. *constant pleasure*] settled decision.
2. *doubted*] feared.
3. *forfended*] forbidden.

103

	Be not familiar with her.
EDM.	Fear me not.— She and the duke her husband!

Enter, with drum and colours, ALBANY, GONERIL, *and* Soldiers

GON.	[*Aside*] I had rather lose the battle than that sister Should loosen him and me.
ALB.	Our very loving sister, well be-met. Sir, this I hear; the king is come to his daughter, With others whom the rigour of our state Forced to cry out. Where I could not be honest, I never yet was valiant: for this business, It toucheth us, as France invades our land, Not bolds the king,[4] with others, whom, I fear, Most just and heavy causes make oppose.
EDM.	Sir, you speak nobly.
REG.	Why is this reason'd?[5]
GON.	Combine together 'gainst the enemy; For these domestic and particular broils Are not the question here.
ALB.	Let's then determine With the ancient of war[6] on our proceedings.
EDM.	I shall attend you presently at your tent.
REG.	Sister, you'll go with us?
GON.	No.
REG.	'T is most convenient; pray you, go with us.
GON.	[*Aside*] O, ho, I know the riddle.—I will go.

As they are going out, enter EDGAR *disguised*

EDG.	If e'er your grace had speech with man so poor, Hear me one word.
ALB.	I'll overtake you. Speak. [*Exeunt all but Albany and Edgar.*]
EDG.	Before you fight the battle, ope this letter.

---

4. *It toucheth us . . . king*] It concerns us not because the French support Lear inasmuch as the French are invading our territory.
5. *reason'd*] discussed, talked about.
6. *ancient of war*] military veterans, those of long experience in warfare.

	If you have victory, let the trumpet sound

If you have victory, let the trumpet sound
For him that brought it: wretched though I seem,
I can produce a champion that will prove
What is avouched there. If you miscarry,
Your business of the world hath so an end,
And machination ceases. Fortune love you!
ALB. Stay till I have read the letter.
EDG.   I was forbid it.
When time shall serve, let but the herald cry,
And I'll appear again.
ALB. Why, fare thee well: I will o'erlook thy paper.

                       [*Exit Edgar.*]

Re-enter Edmund

EDM. The enemy's in view: draw up your powers.
Here is the guess of their true strength and forces
By diligent discovery; but your haste
Is now urged on you.
ALB.   We will greet the time.   [*Exit.*]
EDM. To both these sisters have I sworn my love;
Each jealous of the other, as the stung
Are of the adder. Which of them shall I take?
Both? one? or neither? Neither can be enjoy'd,
If both remain alive: to take the widow
Exasperates, makes mad her sister Goneril;
And hardly shall I carry out my side,[7]
Her husband being alive. Now then we'll use
His countenance for the battle; which being done,
Let her who would be rid of him devise
His speedy taking off. As for the mercy
Which he intends to Lear and to Cordelia,
The battle done, and they within our power,
Shall never see his pardon; for my state
Stands on me to defend, not to debate.   [*Exit.*]

---

7. *carry out my side*] win my game. "Side" is often found as a technical term for a set of partners in a game played by two or more players, and hence was sometimes applied to the game itself or to a bout of play.

SCENE II—*A Field Between the Two Camps*

Alarum within. Enter, with drum and colours, LEAR, CORDELIA, *and* Soldiers, *over the stage; and exeunt*

Enter EDGAR *and* GLOUCESTER

EDG.   Here, father, take the shadow of this tree
            For your good host; pray that the right may thrive:
            If ever I return to you again,
            I'll bring you comfort.
GLOU.   Grace go with you, sir!

                                                    [*Exit Edgar.*]

Alarum and retreat within. Re-enter EDGAR.

EDG.   Away, old man; give me thy hand; away!
            King Lear hath lost, he and his daughter ta'en:
            Give me thy hand; come on.
GLOU.   No further, sir; a man may rot even here.
EDG.   What, in ill thoughts again? Men must endure
            Their going hence, even as their coming hither:
            Ripeness is all: come on.
GLOU.   And that's true too.   [*Exeunt.*]

SCENE III — *The British Camp Near Dover*

Enter, in conquest, with drum and colours, EDMUND; LEAR *and* COR-
DELIA, *as prisoners;* Captain, Soldiers, *etc.*

EDM.   Some officers take them away: good guard,
               Until their greater pleasures first be known
               That are to censure them.
COR.   We are not the first
               Who with best meaning have incurr'd the worst.
               For thee, oppressed king, am I cast down;
               Myself could else out-frown false fortune's frown.
               Shall we not see these daughters and these sisters?
LEAR.   No, no, no, no! Come, let's away to prison:
               We two alone will sing like birds i' the cage:
               When thou dost ask me blessing, I'll kneel down
               And ask of thee forgiveness: so we'll live,
               And pray, and sing, and tell old tales, and laugh
               At gilded butterflies,[1] and hear poor rogues
               Talk of court news; and we'll talk with them too,
               Who loses and who wins, who's in, who's out;
               And take upon 's the mystery of things,
               As if we were God's spies: and we'll wear out,
               In a wall'd prison, packs and sects[2] of great ones
               That ebb and flow by the moon.
EDM.   Take them away.
LEAR.   Upon such sacrifices, my Cordelia,
               The gods themselves throw incense. Have I caught thee?
               He that parts us shall bring a brand from heaven,
               And fire us hence like foxes.[3] Wipe thine eyes;
               The good-years shall devour them, flesh and fell,[4]

---

1. *gilded butterflies*] fashionable courtiers.
2. *packs and sects*] parties and factions (of politicians).
3. *fire us hence like foxes*] drive us away as foxes are expelled from their holes by burning
   them out.
4. *flesh and fell*] literally "flesh and skin"; colloquially used for "flesh and bones."

                Ere they shall make us weep: we'll see 'em starve first.
                Come.   *[Exeunt Lear and Cordelia, guarded.]*

EDM.   Come hither, captain; hark.
                Take thou this note: go follow them to prison:
                One step I have advanced thee; if thou dost
                As this instructs thee, thou dost make thy way
                To noble fortunes: know thou this, that men
                Are as the time is: to be tender-minded
                Does not become a sword: thy great employment
                Will not bear question; either say thou'lt do 't,
                Or thrive by other means.

CAPT.   I'll do 't, my lord.

EDM.   About it; and write happy when thou hast done.
                Mark; I say, instantly, and carry it so
                As I have set it down.

CAPT.   I cannot draw a cart, nor eat dried oats;
                If it be man's work, I'll do 't.   *[Exit.]*

Flourish. Enter ALBANY, GONERIL, REGAN, *another* Captain, *and* Soldiers

ALB.   Sir, you have shown to-day your valiant strain,
                And fortune led you well: you have the captives
                That were the opposites of this day's strife:
                We do require them of you, so to use them
                As we shall find their merits and our safety
                May equally determine.

EDM.   Sir, I thought it fit
                To send the old and miserable king
                To some retention and appointed guard;
                Whose age has charms in it, whose title more,
                To pluck the common bosom on his side,
                And turn our impress'd lances[5] in our eyes
                Which do command them. With him I sent the queen:
                My reason all the same; and they are ready
                To-morrow or at further space to appear
                Where you shall hold your session. At this time
                We sweat and bleed: the friend hath lost his friend;

---

5. *our impress'd lances*] weapons of the men we have impressed into our service.

        And the best quarrels, in the heat, are cursed
        By those that feel their sharpness.[6]
        The question of Cordelia and her father
        Requires a fitter place.

ALB.   Sir, by your patience,
        I hold you but a subject of this war,
        Not as a brother.

REG.   That's as we list to grace him.
        Methinks our pleasure might have been demanded,
        Ere you had spoke so far. He led our powers,
        Bore the commission of my place and person;
        The which immediacy may well stand up
        And call itself your brother.

GON.   Not so hot:
        In his own grace he doth exalt himself
        More than in your addition.[7]

REG.   In my rights,
        By me invested, he compeers the best.

GON.   That were the most, if he should husband you.

REG.   Jesters do oft prove prophets.

GON.   Holla, holla!
        That eye that told you so look'd but a-squint.

REG.   Lady, I am not well; else I should answer
        From a full-flowing stomach.[8] General,
        Take thou my soldiers, prisoners, patrimony;
        Dispose of them, of me; the walls are thine:[9]
        Witness the world, that I create thee here
        My lord and master.

GON.   Mean you to enjoy him?

ALB.   The let-alone[10] lies not in your good will.

EDM.   Nor in thine, lord.

ALB.   Half-blooded fellow, yes.

---

6. *And the best quarrels . . . sharpness*] And those engaged in wars even when waged in the justest of causes curse the quarrel when they suffer the bitter consequences, (either from loss of friends or by reason of their own wounds).

7. *in your addition*] by virtue of the title with which you invest him.

8. *stomach*] anger.

9. *The walls are thine*] Regan surrenders her person as though it were a vanquished citadel.

10. *let-alone*] prohibition.

REG.   [*To Edmund*] Let the drum strike, and prove my title thine.
ALB.   Stay yet; hear reason. Edmund, I arrest thee
            On capital treason; and in thine attaint[11]
            This gilded serpent [*pointing to Gon.*]. For your claim, fair sister,
            I bar it in the interest of my wife;
            'T is she is sub-contracted to this lord,
            And I, her husband, contradict your bans.
            If you will marry, make your loves to me;
            My lady is bespoke.
GON.   An interlude![12]
ALB.   Thou art arm'd, Gloucester: let the trumpet sound:
            If none appear to prove upon thy person
            Thy heinous, manifest, and many treasons,
            There is my pledge [*throwing down a glove*]: I'll prove it on thy
                heart,
            Ere I taste bread, thou art in nothing less
            Than I have here proclaim'd thee.
REG.   Sick, O, sick!
GON.   [*Aside*] If not, I'll ne'er trust medicine.[13]
EDM.   [*Throwing down a glove*] There's my exchange: what in the
                world he is
            That names me traitor, villain-like he lies:
            Call by thy trumpet: he that dares approach,
            On him, on you, — who not? — I will maintain
            My truth and honour firmly.
ALB.   A herald, ho!
EDM.   A herald, ho, a herald!
ALB.   Trust to thy single virtue;[14] for thy soldiers,
            All levied in my name, have in my name
            Took their discharge.
REG.   My sickness grows upon me.
ALB.   She is not well; convey her to my tent.
                                                [*Exit Regan, led.*]

Enter a Herald

---

11. *in thine attaint*] in connection with thy impeachment.
12. *An interlude!*] A farce is on foot!
13. *I'll ne'er trust medicine*] Goneril has poisoned Regan.
14. *thy single virtue*] thy personal valour.

        Come hither, herald, — Let the trumpet sound, —
        And read out this.

CAPT.   Sound, trumpet!   *[A trumpet sounds.]*

HER.   *[Reads]* "If any man of quality or degree within the lists of the army
     will maintain upon Edmund, supposed Earl of Gloucester, that he is a
     manifold traitor, let him appear by the third sound of the trumpet: he is
     bold in his defence."

EDM.   Sound!   *[First trumpet.]*

HER.   Again!   *[Second trumpet.]*

HER.   Again!   *[Third trumpet.]*
                                    [Trumpet answers within.]

Enter EDGAR, *at the third sound, armed, with a trumpet before him*

ALB.   Ask him his purposes, why he appears
     Upon this call o' the trumpet.

HER.   What are you?
     Your name, your quality? and why you answer
     This present summons?

EDG.   Know, my name is lost;
     By treason's tooth bare-gnawn and canker-bit:[15]
     Yet am I noble as the adversary
     I come to cope.[16]

ALB.   Which is that adversary?

EDG.   What's he that speaks for Edmund, Earl of Gloucester?

EDM.   Himself: what say'st thou to him?

EDG.   Draw thy sword,
     That if my speech offend a noble heart,
     Thy arm may do thee justice: here is mine.
     Behold, it is the privilege of mine honours,
     My oath, and my profession: I protest,
     Maugre[17] thy strength, youth, place and eminence,
     Despite thy victor sword and fire-new fortune,
     Thy valour and thy heart, thou art a traitor,
     False to thy gods, thy brother and thy father,
     Conspirant 'gainst this high illustrious prince,

---

15. *canker-bit*] bitten by the caterpillar, by vermin.
16. *cope*] encounter.
17. *Maugre*] in spite of.

And from the extremest upward of thy head
To the descent and dust below thy foot,
A most toad-spotted traitor. Say thou "No,"
This sword, this arm and my best spirits are bent
To prove upon thy heart, whereto I speak,
Thou liest.

EDM.   In wisdom I should ask thy name,
But since thy outside looks so fair and warlike
And that thy tongue some say of breeding breathes,
What safe and nicely I might well delay
By rule of knighthood,[18] I disdain and spurn:
Back do I toss these treasons to thy head;
With the hell-hated[19] lie o'erwhelm thy heart;
Which for they yet glance by and scarcely bruise.
This sword of mine shall give them instant way,
Where they shall rest for ever. Trumpets, speak!
                    [*Alarums. They fight. Edmund falls.*]

ALB.   Save him, save him!
GON.   This is practice,[20] Gloucester:
By the law of arms thou wast not bound to answer
An unknown opposite; thou art not vanquish'd,
But cozen'd and beguiled.
ALB.   Shut your mouth, dame,
Or with this paper shall I stop it. Hold, sir;
Thou worse than any name, read thine own evil.
No tearing, lady; I perceive you know it.
GON.   Say, if I do, the laws are mine, not thine:
Who can arraign me for 't?
ALB.   Most monstrous!
Know'st thou this paper?
GON.   Ask me not what I know.   [*Exit.*]
ALB.   Go after her: she's desperate; govern her.
EDM.   What you have charged me with, that have I done;
And more, much more; the time will bring it out:

---

18. *What safe . . . knighthood*] That refusal (of your challenge) which I might well and
   quite accurately make in accordance with the laws of chivalry.
19. *hell-hated*] hated as hell.
20. *practice*] deceitful intrigue.

'T is past, and so am I. But what art thou
That hast this fortune on me? If thou 'rt noble,
I do forgive thee.

EDG.   Let's exchange charity.
I am no less in blood than thou art, Edmund;
If more, the more thou hast wrong'd me.
My name is Edgar, and thy father's son.
The gods are just, and of our pleasant vices
Make instruments to plague us:
The dark and vicious place where thee he got
Cost him his eyes.

EDM.   Thou hast spoken right, 't is true;
The wheel is come full circle; I am here.

ALB.   Methought thy very gait did prophesy
A royal nobleness: I must embrace thee:
Let sorrow split my heart, if ever I
Did hate thee or thy father!

EDG.   Worthy prince, I know't.

ALB.   Where have you hid yourself?
How have you known the miseries of your father?

EDG.   By nursing them, my lord. List a brief tale;
And when 't is told, O, that my heart would burst!
The bloody proclamation to escape
That follow'd me so near, — O, our lives' sweetness!
That we the pain of death would hourly die
Rather than die at once![21] — taught me to shift
Into a madman's rags, to assume a semblance
That very dogs disdain'd: and in this habit
Met I my father with his bleeding rings,[22]
Their precious stones new lost; became his guide,
Led him, begg'd for him, saved him from despair;
Never — O fault! — reveal'd myself unto him,
Until some half-hour past, when I was arm'd;
Not sure, though hoping, of this good success,
I ask'd his blessing, and from first to last

---

21. *we the pain . . . die at once*] we would suffer every hour the pain of death rather than die once for all.
22. *rings*] sockets of the eyes.

Told him my pilgrimage: but his flaw'd heart,—
Alack, too weak the conflict to support!—
'Twixt two extremes of passion, joy and grief,
Burst smilingly.

EDM.   This speech of yours hath moved me,
And shall perchance do good: but speak you on;
You look as you had something more to say.

ALB.   If there be more, more woful, hold it in;
For I am almost ready to dissolve,
Hearing of this.

EDG.   This would have seem'd a period
To such as love not sorrow; but another,
To amplify too much, would make much more,
And top extremity.[23]
Whilst I was big in clamour, came there in a man,
Who, having seen me in my worst estate,
Shunn'd my abhorr'd society; but then, finding
Who 't was that so endured, with his strong arms
He fasten'd on my neck, and bellow'd out
As he'ld burst heaven; threw him on my father;
Told the most piteous tale of Lear and him
That ever ear received: which in recounting
His grief grew puissant, and the strings of life
Began to crack: twice then the trumpets sounded,
And there I left him tranced.

ALB.   But who was this?

EDG.   Kent, sir, the banish'd Kent; who in disguise
Follow'd his enemy king, and did him service
Improper for a slave.

Enter a Gentleman, *with a bloody knife*

GENT.   Help, help, O, help!

EDG.   What kind of help?

ALB.   Speak, man.

EDG.   What means this bloody knife?

GENT.   'T is hot, it smokes;

---

23. *but another . . . extremity*] Any further period or conclusion to my story, by adding
sorrow to what is already too much, would substantially increase the pathos and exceed
the utmost limits of grief.

	It came even from the heart of — O, she's dead!
ALB.	Who dead? speak, man.
GENT.	Your lady, sir, your lady: and her sister
	By her is poisoned; she hath confess'd it.
EDM.	I was contracted to them both: all three
	Now marry in an instant.
EDG.	Here comes Kent.
ALB.	Produce the bodies, be they alive or dead.

[Exit Gentleman.]

This judgement of the heavens, that makes us tremble,
Touches us not with pity.

Enter Kent

O, is this he?

The time will not allow the compliment
Which very manners urges.

KENT.	I am come
	To bid my king and master aye good night:
	Is he not here?
ALB.	Great thing of us forgot!
	Speak, Edmund, where's the king? and where's Cordelia?
	See'st thou this object, Kent?

[The bodies of Goneril and Regan are brought in.]

KENT.	Alack, why thus?
EDM.	Yet Edmund was beloved:
	The one the other poison'd for my sake,
	And after slew herself.
ALB.	Even so. Cover their faces.
EDM.	I pant for life: some good I mean to do,
	Despite of mine own nature. Quickly send,
	Be brief in it, to the castle; for my writ
	Is on the life of Lear and on Cordelia:
	Nay, send in time.
ALB.	Run, run, O, run!
EDG.	To who, my lord? Who hath the office? send
	Thy token of reprieve.
EDM.	Well thought on: take my sword,
	Give it the captain.
ALB.	Haste thee, for thy life. *[Exit Edgar.]*

EDM.	He hath commission from thy wife and me
	To hang Cordelia in the prison, and
	To lay the blame upon her own despair,
	That she fordid herself.[24]
ALB.	The gods defend her! Bear him hence awhile.

[*Edmund is borne off.*]

Re-enter LEAR, *with* CORDELIA *dead in his arms*; EDGAR, Captain, *and others following*

LEAR.	Howl, howl, howl, howl! O, you are men of stones:
	Had I your tongues and eyes, I'ld use them so
	That heaven's vault should crack. She's gone for ever:
	I know when one is dead and when one lives;
	She's dead as earth. Lend me a looking-glass;
	If that her breath will mist or stain the stone,[25]
	Why, then she lives.
KENT.	Is this the promised end?
EDG.	Or image of that horror?
ALB.	Fall and cease.
LEAR.	This feather stirs; she lives. If it be so,
	It is a chance which does redeem all sorrows
	That ever I have felt.
KENT.	[*Kneeling*] O my good master!
LEAR.	Prithee, away.
EDG.	'T is noble Kent, your friend.
LEAR.	A plague upon you, murderers, traitors all!
	I might have saved her; now she's gone for ever!
	Cordelia, Cordelia! stay a little. Ha!
	What is't thou say'st? Her voice was ever soft,
	Gentle and low, an excellent thing in woman.
	I kill'd the slave that was a-hanging thee.
CAPT.	'T is true, my lords, he did.
LEAR.	Did I not, fellow?
	I have seen the day, with my good biting falchion[26]
	I would have made them skip: I am old now,

24. *fordid herself*] destroyed herself.
25. *the stone*] the mirror of crystal.
26. *falchion*] scimitar.

And these same crosses[27] spoil me. Who are you?
Mine eyes are not o' the best: I'll tell you straight.

KENT.   If fortune brag of two she loved and hated,
One of them we behold.

LEAR.   This is a dull sight. Are you not Kent?

KENT.   The same,
Your servant Kent. Where is your servant Caius?

LEAR.   He's a good fellow, I can tell you that;
He'll strike, and quickly too: he's dead and rotten.

KENT.   No, my good lord; I am the very man —

LEAR.   I'll see that straight.

KENT.   That from your first of difference[28] and decay
Have follow'd your sad steps.

LEAR.   You are welcome hither.

KENT.   Nor no man else: all's cheerless, dark and deadly.
Your eldest daughters have fordone themselves,
And desperately[29] are dead.

LEAR.   Ay, so I think.

ALB.   He knows not what he says, and vain is it
That we present us to him.

EDG.   Very bootless.

Enter a Captain

CAPT.   Edmund is dead, my lord.

ALB.   That's but a trifle here.
You lords and noble friends, know our intent.
What comfort to this great decay may come
Shall be applied: for us, we will resign,
During the life of this old majesty,
To him our absolute power: [*To Edgar and Kent*] you, to your
        rights;
With boot, and such addition as your honours
Have more than merited. All friends shall taste

---

27. *crosses*] misadventures.
28. *from your first of difference*] from the first indication of your change of fortune.
29. *desperately*] in the despair of sin which denies them salvation.

	The wages of their virtue, and all foes
	The cup of their deservings. O, see, see!
LEAR.	And my poor fool[30] is hang'd! No, no, no life!
	Why should a dog, a horse, a rat, have life,
	And thou no breath at all? Thou'lt come no more,
	Never, never, never, never, never!
	Pray you, undo this button: thank you, sir.
	Do you see this? Look on her, look, her lips,
	Look there, look there! [*Dies.*]
EDG.	He faints. My lord, my lord!
KENT.	Break, heart; I prithee, break!
EDG.	Look up, my lord.
KENT.	Vex not his ghost: O, let him pass! he hates him
	That would upon the rack of this tough world
	Stretch him out longer.
EDG.	He is gone indeed.
KENT.	The wonder is he hath endured so long:
	He but usurp'd his life.
ALB.	Bear them from hence. Our present business
	Is general woe. [*To Kent and Edgar*] Friends of my soul, you twain
	Rule in this realm and the gored state sustain.
KENT.	I have a journey, sir, shortly to go;
	My master calls me, I must not say no.
ALB.	The weight of this sad time we must obey,
	Speak what we feel, not what we ought to say.
	The oldest hath borne most: we that are young
	Shall never see so much, nor live so long.

[*Exeunt, with a dead march.*]

---

30. *my poor fool*] a common term of endearment, here applied by Lear to Cordelia.

DOVER · THRIFT · EDITIONS

All books complete and unabridged. All 5³⁄₁₆″ × 8¼″, paperbound.
Just $1.00–$2.00 in U.S.A.

A selection of the more than 100 titles in the series:

FLATLAND: A ROMANCE OF MANY DIMENSIONS, Edwin A. Abbott. 96pp. 27263-X $1.00

DOVER BEACH AND OTHER POEMS, Matthew Arnold. 112pp. 28037-3 $1.00

CIVIL WAR STORIES, Ambrose Bierce. 128pp. 28038-1 $1.00

THE DEVIL'S DICTIONARY, Ambrose Bierce. 144pp. 27542-6 $1.00

SONGS OF INNOCENCE AND SONGS OF EXPERIENCE, William Blake. 64pp. 27051-3 $1.00

SONNETS FROM THE PORTUGUESE AND OTHER POEMS, Elizabeth Barrett Browning. 64pp.
27052-1 $1.00

MY LAST DUCHESS AND OTHER POEMS, Robert Browning. 128pp. 27783-6 $1.00

SELECTED POEMS, George Gordon, Lord Byron. 112pp. 27784-4 $1.00

ALICE'S ADVENTURES IN WONDERLAND, Lewis Carroll. 96pp. 27543-4 $1.00

O PIONEERS!, Willa Cather. 128pp. 27785-2 $1.00

THE CHERRY ORCHARD, Anton Chekhov. 64pp. 26682-6 $1.00

THE AWAKENING, Kate Chopin. 128pp. 27786-0 $1.00

THE RIME OF THE ANCIENT MARINER AND OTHER POEMS, Samuel Taylor Coleridge. 80pp.
27266-4 $1.00

HEART OF DARKNESS, Joseph Conrad. 80pp. 26464-5 $1.00

THE RED BADGE OF COURAGE, Stephen Crane. 112pp. 26465-3 $1.00

A CHRISTMAS CAROL, Charles Dickens. 80pp. 26865-9 $1.00

THE CRICKET ON THE HEARTH AND OTHER CHRISTMAS STORIES, Charles Dickens. 128pp.
28039-X $1.00

SELECTED POEMS, Emily Dickinson. 64pp. 26466-1 $1.00

SELECTED POEMS, John Donne. 96pp. 27788-7 $1.00

NOTES FROM THE UNDERGROUND, Fyodor Dostoyevsky. 96pp. 27053-X $1.00

SIX GREAT SHERLOCK HOLMES STORIES, Sir Arthur Conan Doyle. 112pp. 27055-6 $1.00

THE SOULS OF BLACK FOLK, W. E. B. Du Bois. 176pp. 28041-1 $2.00

MEDEA, Euripides. 64pp. 27548-5 $1.00

A BOY'S WILL AND NORTH OF BOSTON, Robert Frost. 112pp. (Available in U.S. only)
26866-7 $1.00

WHERE ANGELS FEAR TO TREAD, E. M. Forster. 128pp. (Available in U.S. only) 27791-7
$1.00

FAUST, PART ONE, Johann Wolfgang von Goethe. 192pp. 28046-2 $2.00

THE SCARLET LETTER, Nathaniel Hawthorne. 192pp. 28048-9 $2.00

A DOLL'S HOUSE, Henrik Ibsen. 80pp. 27062-9 $1.00

THE TURN OF THE SCREW, Henry James. 96pp. 26684-2 $1.00

VOLPONE, Ben Jonson. 112pp. 28049-7 $1.00

DUBLINERS, James Joyce. 160pp. 26870-5 $1.00

A PORTRAIT OF THE ARTIST AS A YOUNG MAN, James Joyce. 192pp. 28050-0 $2.00

LYRIC POEMS, John Keats. 80pp. 26871-3 $1.00

THE BOOK OF PSALMS, King James Bible. 144pp. 27541-8 $1.00